WELCOME TO THE INFERNO

DANIEL PARME

This is a work of fiction. Names, characters, places, and incidents are products of the author's imagination and are not to be construed as real. Any resemblance to actual events, locales, organizations, or persons, living or dead, is entirely coincidental.

Well, Anthony Bourdain was a real person… The Bourdain in this book merely *looks* like the real Bourdain. The rest is an invention of the author.

© Daniel Parme, 2023
Published by Last-Picked Books
Pittsburgh, PA
lastpickedbooks.com

Cover by Daniel Parme.
Devil face painted by Juan Machaca, *Street Talent Galeria Oaxaca*

All rights reserved. No part of this publication may be used or reproduced without written permission except in the case of brief quotations embodied in critical articles and reviews.

For everyone
who's ever found themselves
deep in the bowels
of the service industry.

You can always tell when a person has worked in a restaurant. There's an empathy that can only be cultivated by those who've stood between a hungry mouth and a $28 pork chop, a special understanding of the way a bunch of motley misfits can be a family. Service industry work develops the "soft skills" recruiters talk about on LinkedIn — discipline, promptness, the ability to absorb criticism, and most important, how to read people like a book. The work is thankless and fun and messy, and the world would be a kinder place if more people tried it. With all due respect to my former professors, I've long believed I gained more knowledge in kitchens, bars, and dining rooms than any college could even hold.

~ Anthony Bourdain

Hope not ever to see Heaven.
I have come to lead you to the other shore;
into eternal darkness; into fire and into ice.

~ Dante Alighieri: *Inferno*

ONE

This fucking business, man.

I'd just finished working a double—a true double, open to close, first one in for lunch, last non-manager out the door at night—and as you might expect, I needed a drink. The rest of the staff were meeting up at our usual spot, but I'd just spent fourteen hours with those people, and I needed a break from them every bit as much as I did from the customers. So I headed the opposite direction, to a pizza shop with a bar on the second floor and a veteran bartender I considered to be one of the best in the business. Amy was always happy to help me decompress with a drink and an understanding ear. She'd been in the industry even longer than I had, and over time she'd become my favorite person to commiserate with. She also had possibly the best ass in the business, but that's a discussion for another time.

This particular double had been so trying because of the massive country music festival at the stadium just across the river. If you've never experienced this kind of crowd, you are a truly blessed individual.

Now, I'm not saying *all* country music fans are drunken buffoons with a combined IQ no higher than the teased bangs of '90s-era Reba McEntire, but today it certainly seemed that way. I'd had to refuse service to two groups of them during the dinner rush. Neither group took it well, of course, and I'm sure there will be a couple negative online reviews about it, but at least they didn't break anything on their way out.

Now several hours later, my quest for a bourbon and a beer made it plain that although the show had been over for quite a while, these people were nowhere near the end of their evening. You wouldn't believe the hootin' and hollerin', the open groping and drunk-on-the-streets-of-downtown making out.

And let us not forget the insane amount of trash littering the streets: fast food wrappers containing half-eaten devoured double cheeseburgers; shattered bottles and crushed cans in little pools of beer; empty cans of chew; innumerable red Solo cups balanced on every nearly-flat surface, threatening to drown the city in a tsunami of spilled tobacco spit.

They were everywhere, a sea of cowboy boots and hats, of denim and Confederate flags, of Budweiser-fueled racism and bigotry.

And tragically, though perhaps predictably, I got to the pizza shop to find a large group of them clustered directly in front of the doors, which meant the bar inside was probably fucking packed. But I wanted that drink, dammit, so I put my head down, uttered a few unheard *excuse me*'s, and tried to force my way through.

"Look at this fuckin' guy," belched out a star-spangled pickup of a man as he stepped intentionally into my path. A few of the others grunted with recognition and circled around me, walling me in.

"Come on, guys," I said, opening my hands in front of me, a gesture of peace. "I'm just trying to get a drink."

Flag-man laughed and gave my shoulder a little shove. "Oh I'm sorry, but I don't think we can help you."

"Seems like you've already had enough," said one of the guys behind me.

"Gonna have to take your business somewhere else," chimed in another.

I probably should have looked at their faces before now, but years of working downtown had taught me to avoid after-midnight eye contact at nearly any cost. By now it was habit, and good habit at that, but even the best habits can have less than the best consequences. If I'd looked before entering the fray, I'd have realized this was one of the groups I'd denied service to earlier. I'd have realized it, and I'd have turned around to join the rest of my staff for that drink.

Instead, I found myself surrounded by this invading army of plastered post-show country bros, country bros I'd jilted at the bar only hours ago, and I knew immediately that this was not going to end well. I'd end up drinking that beer with, at best, only some chew spit dribbling down my front, at worst, probably a black eye, maybe a busted lip.

But then a potential savior, clad in denim daisy dukes and a sleeveless flannel shirt knotted just below a pierced belly button, forced her way into the circle. "Come on, you guys, knock it off," she said, planting herself between Flag-man and me and, resting a comforting hand on my arm, flashing me a reassuring and lovely little smile. "He was only doing his job, Bo. And we *were* already drunk. I mean, we started drinking at breakfast."

Bo, formerly known as Flag-man, spat, narrowly missing my black slip-resistant shoes with his thick brown foulness. "Fuck that, Lauren. The customer's *always* right, right? I was just gonna leave a bad Yelp review tomorrow, but maybe we should just teach him a lesson now, since he's here."

A few chuckles from the group, and a shove from behind sent me falling forward into Lauren, who fell into Bo, knocking the Solo cup of tobacco spit from his hand, spilling it down his jeans and onto his cowboy boots.

"The fuck, man?!" he growled as he inspected his soiled pants. "You think that's cool? Pushing a fucking chick?" He then, utterly unaware of the irony, shoved Lauren to the side to get a clear line at me.

So it was to be the busted lip for me, then. Unless I could charm my way out of it, of course, which was entirely possible. I'd talked my way out of worse. "Come on, man. Your boy sh—"

I couldn't finish my thought because he suckered me in the stomach, knocking the wind out of me and doubling me over.

Lauren jumped back between us. "Bo! Stop! He

didn't—"

But he shoved his way past her again, then pushed me again. His boys must have stepped out of the way, because instead of bumping into the guy behind me like I'd expected to, I crashed into an overstuffed trash can and spun into the car parked along the curb behind it. Bracing myself with my hands against the hood, I was still trying to catch my breath as he grabbed my backpack and spun me back around to face him, his friends laughing and cheering him on while Lauren kept slapping him on the back, pleading for him to stop.

"Fuckin' city fuck," he said, either ignoring or oblivious to Lauren's pleas and now holding me by the straps of my backpack. "With your stupid fucking Star Wars tie. Nerd. Not so much better than us now, are you?"

This now sounded like it had very little to do with me, but I still couldn't find my breath to say so, no matter how deeply that dig about my TIE Fighter tie stung. My silence might as well have been an invitation. Without another word he caught me across the chin, sending me toppling over the hood of the car and into the street. I got to my knees, but immediately something struck me in the back, sending me back to the pavement, where I cracked my head and promptly blacked out.

When I came to, I looked up to find a hand reaching down for my own. Without thinking, I took it and allowed its owner to pull me off the street. "You're all right, kid," the man said, in a voice I thought I knew. "Come on. You got places to be."

I was still a little woozy, so it took a minute to focus,

to see his face clearly. I knew I knew that voice. This man was, unmistakably, Anthony fucking Bourdain, all six-foot-whatever of him, lanky-ass arms and legs, little golden hoop through his left earlobe. One of my heroes. Fucking awesome, right?

Only problem was that he'd died a couple years earlier.

"Uh, thanks, man."

He smiled, and it seemed genuine enough. "Don't worry about it, kid. All I did was help you up, though. It's not like I saved your life or anything."

"That's true, I guess. But still, thanks." I looked at my watch, but it must have broken when I fell. "Shit. It was great to meet you, Mr. Bourdain, but I really gotta get to work."

I managed only two steps before careening into yet another parked car.

He steadied me and looked over my shoulder at his reflection in the window. "Bourdain, huh? Yeah I can work with this." Then he turned his attention back to me. "Work? From the look of it, I'd say you've already put in one hell of a shift today. And you took a nasty little shot to the head back there. Might wanna let me walk with you, make sure you don't pass out or anything. Concussions are no joke."

"Oh. Yeah, okay," I said as he led me around the corner, suddenly remembering the crowd and the drunk woman, the Flag-man and the punching. "Where are those fuckin'—?"

I started to turn around to get a look, but Tony urged me forward. "Oh they took off as soon as the car hit you," he said, removing his hand after I gave in and continued walking. "Asshole just kept on driving, too."

I stopped and looked at him, still a little dazed. "Shouldn't I go back and file a report or something?"

"I'm sure somebody got it all on video. You can always go to the cops later, if you think that'll accomplish anything. For now, let's get you back to work, dig out the first aid kit. Or at least get some ice for your head."

I thought for a moment. "I, uh, I don't have keys."

"Don't worry about that right now. We'll figure something out," he said. Then, with a half-chuckle, "What were you thinking back there, anyway? Not that it's any of my business, but didn't you expect something like that to happen? Probably should have just put your head down and gone on to the next place."

I still couldn't quite figure out what he was doing there. I mean, bumping into a celebrity at two in the morning in downtown Pittsburgh isn't exactly a common occurrence, but it was something more than that. Plus, my head—it didn't hurt, exactly, but I was far from comfortable. Otherwise, I like to think I'd have been a little less snippy with my food service hero. "Expect something like what? Getting my ass beat by some random redneck asshole? Can't say the possibility really ever crossed my mind." I opened my mouth wide to pop my sore jaw, rubbed my swelling chin. "You're right, though. I should've taken off the second they recognized me."

"Yeah, I've been there, kid," he said with a little pat on my back. Then he really got going. "People, particularly us over-educated Yankees, will tell you everyone from the South is at least a bit of a yokel. From their love of peasant food—and let's be honest here, it's slave food—pickled pigs feet, collards, grits drowning in lard or pig fat—to their hatred of abortion, immigrants, and vegans. Their adoration of all things gun.

"The Mason-Dixon Line is so much more than merely an imaginary line separating the Union from the Confederacy. It's as close to a literal line in the sand as we can get when it comes to the viewpoint that there is more that separates us than there is that unites us as freedom-loving citizens of this supposedly great nation.

"But in my mind, the far greater, thicker, more substantial line in the sand is the one drawn between country fans and the rest of us. We lovers of all things non-country—blues, rock, hip hop, soul, almost any genre of music, really—which, to be fair, modern country has begun to incorporate, whether or not the fans appreciate or even realize it—we look down, probably unfairly, on this vapid form of music with its lyrics of trucks and dogs and beer and boots-in-asses and unfaithful women.

"But why? All music is centered on the human experience, and who amongst us has never loved a dog, a woman or a man, or a particular vehicle? It's not the actual music that divides us so. It's something more. Something deeper.

"The way fans of sports teams refuse to visit the city that houses their greatest rival. It's almost feudal. Like the city-states of ancient Greece, fighting their never-ending wars, leaving death and destruction in their wake all for the love of Sparta, all for a sense of pride that is all too fleeting when it really comes down to it. In reality, we're all waging the same war, fighting the same battle to distinguish ourselves in this world of sameness and mediocrity.

"It's not country music, or even country music fans, that are the enemy, but the system that aims to divide us, to see one another as villains, as *other*, when all we really are is people with varying tastes and personalities." He stopped dead and pulled a surprised look, eyes narrowed and head tilted, and he shook his head. "Man, what the hell was that?"

"What was what?"

"Every time I visit, I forget what it's like to assume the…You know what? Nevermind."

"Yeah," I finally said, still processing his little rant, still confused. "Not to be, you know, rude, but aren't you dead?"

"What's that?"

"I mean, you, uh…it was all over the news, man."

He harumphed. "You always believe what you see on the news?"

"Well, I guess that did sound like you. That whole monologue-y thing, I mean. I just…I didn't realize you talked like that all the time. Kinda thought it was just for the books or the tv shows. Don't get me wrong. I'm a huge fan. It's just a little weird."

"Fan? What are…Oh, right. *Bourdain*," he chuckled. "Yeah. I'm here for a shoot, you know? Mind's on my work. It happens. I mean, I'm sure you accidentally slip into bartender-voice sometimes, right? Outside of work?"

I considered. Bartender-voice—customer-service-voice in any of its forms, really—is a sort of mask that protects you from becoming your job, if you catch my meaning. Like using this different voice is the only reason you're able to hold onto yourself, who you really are, so you don't allow yourself to be overtaken by this role you're playing, so you don't allow yourself to become merely *the help*. It's a valuable tool to carry around in your apron. Sometimes, though, that voice becomes so comfortable, so second nature, that it slips out in the rest of your life. There's just no helping it.

"Yeah," I said. "It definitely happens."

"Same shit," he said. "After a while, it's like the part you play becomes a part of who you are, you know?"

"Guess I can't argue with that," I said, having experienced this phenomenon fairly often, even losing a couple of relationships because of it. "How'd you know I was a bartender?"

"I've been doing this for a very, very long time, kid. After a while, it's like you can smell it on a person."

I'd experienced this one, too, many times. Food service people have... *a way*, I guess? You don't need to have worked with a person, or sometimes even spoken to them, to know they're part of the family. You can just sense it, or see it in their eyes, or whatever. I know how it sounds, but it's the fucking truth.

I was about to say as much, but then we were there, approaching the front door of the restaurant. The lights were off, and it seemed the manager had gone for the night. I reached for the door handle, to give it a tug, just to be sure, and then I noticed it: the door. We were in the right place, but it wasn't the right door. It should have been one of those boring metal-framed things with a push-bar and finger-smudged glass, a sign with the hours hanging from a suction-cupped hook on the inside, the outside etched with our name and logo.

This door was, and had, none of those things. This door was ancient wood, stained with time and weather and god knows what else, and at least four feet taller. No hours were posted. No logo. Just a heavy, rusty metal ring where the deadbolt should have been, and a wooden sign hanging from a fraying rope that read, in hand-painted letters, *Abandon all hope, ye who enter here.*

There was something subtly different about the frame, as well. Whereas ours was some sort of alloy painted black, this appeared to be made of stone. And it didn't really look like a door frame, either. It was this cartoonish yet somehow terrifying carving of what I can only assume was meant to be Satan, crazy-eyes, gnarled teeth and horns and all, mouth stretched open wide to accommodate that magnificent door and whoever might walk through it.

I stood there and stared at it for I don't know how long. I was, to be perfectly honest, dumbfounded.

I looked up and down the street, and everything else seemed to be the same: neon signs advertising crappy beers in the windows of the neighboring shithole, a horde of people smoking cigarettes while waiting for the bus across the street, that missing brick in the sidewalk about a foot from the trashcan, the kind with the ashtray on top.

"You all right there, kid?"

I shook my head, not like saying no, but like trying to shake this unholy vision from my retinas. "This, uh…I don't know. I mean, um…maybe I should go to the hospital."

"The door?"

"Yeah. The door. It's not—wait. You see it, too?"

"Well, yeah. It's right there, horns and all."

"But, there aren't horns on…I mean…that's not…" I looked up and down the street again. "Everything else is… I mean, what the fuck is this?" I looked at him for help, not because I thought he'd have any idea what was going on here, but because he was who was there, and I needed someone.

"Mr. Bourdain," I continued, calming myself so I wouldn't look like a frightened rabbit in front of my hero, who just happened to know how best to cook a frightened rabbit, along with an excellent *beurre noisette*. "You really see it, too?"

He lowered his head, sighed, and looked back up at me. "I do," he said. "And I'm gonna need you to trust me here, kid."

I stared at him, my mind so overloaded it went blank.

He grabbed the rusted metal ring, which glowed a menacing red at his touch, and pulled that massive door open like it was nothing. I peeked in but didn't see my bar, or the dining room, or the host stand.

What I saw was nothing.

And I don't mean *nothing* as in *the lack of something*, either. What I saw was definitely *something*, like dark matter in space, intangible yet all-encompassing in its thereness.

"Trust you?" I asked, staring into this non-thing.

"I know," said Tony. "It's a little fucked up."

"Uh, yeah. No fucking way I'm walking into whatever the fuck that is."

Tony sighed again, this time way more pronounced, like it was *at* me, the way I sigh when I'm far enough from my most grating regulars that they won't hear me as they pull up a seat at the other end of the bar. He wasn't the only one who'd been doing this a long time. I knew that sigh.

"Look," he said. "I'm not here on a shoot, okay? I'm here for you."

I didn't budge, didn't even blink. I was gonna stand there, cold and steadfast, until he started to make sense.

"I'm not even really *Mr. Bourdain*. I'm…someone else. But none of that really matters. The thing is, we really need to get going. I promise I'll explain on the way."

"On the way where?"

"Bloody hell. Just walk through the door already, all right?"

I crossed my arms, stood my ground.

"Look," he said like he'd hoped it wouldn't have come to this, "You're either hallucinating, and none of this is real, so coming with me won't matter when you come back to reality, or this is very real and you're about to learn about things you never imagined possible. If it's a dream or whatever…well, whatever then, right? I mean, you wake up and everything's back to normal. If it's real, though—I mean, come on, do you really want to spend another twenty or thirty years waiting on these assholes?"

I peered into the nothingness again, then back to Tony.

"Fuck it," I said, either too pissed off about the events of the day, or too concussed, to take some time to think it over.

"My man!" he said. "I had a feeling you'd—"

But I lost his voice as I walked through that gaping, fanged devil mouth and allowed it to swallow me whole.

TWO

The door slammed closed behind us more forcefully than it should have. Looked like the thing was solid wood, probably something heavy like oak. But it sounded like one of those massive metal doors they use to hide top secret military fighter jets in the movies, meant not only to keep dangerous secrets locked inside, but also to keep dangerous people out. The kind of closing that means it won't be opening again anytime soon.

It was loud as hell, but only for a moment. There was no hint of an echo. There was, I felt, nothing. No walls to bounce back the sound, no floor on which to stand—though I was fairly certain I was standing—and no light. No light, but not any darkness, either. Darker than darkness, this place, and a silence I'd never thought possible. The kind of nothing that made my existence feel utterly insignificant, like my being there somehow made that place even less whole, like I wasn't even there. Like maybe Mister fucking Bourdain wasn't there, either.

"Mr. Bourdain?"

Nothing. I spun, suddenly wildly terrified I'd be forced to face this place alone.

"Mr. Bourdain?!"

Again, nothing. Moments? Seconds? Minutes? I mean, probably not minutes, but time distortion is a real thing, so I guess maybe? But it felt like a long fucking time I stood there, straining all my senses, trying to pick up, well, anything.

"Beside you," he said, sudden and calm like walking an appetizer to a table during the rush.

If I'd been carrying a tray laden with drinks, I'd have dropped it. Things being as they were, I just jumped a little. "Jesus Christ! Don't do that," I said, half-afraid the void would swallow my voice. "Where are we?"

"Give it a second."

"Give what a second?"

"It's easier if you just see it."

Speaking to an apparently spectral being who seems perfectly at home in the utter absence of everything is incredibly frustrating, especially when you're dangerously close to shitting yourself. "Goddammit. Easier if I just see what?"

"Is it gonna be like this the whole time with you, kid?" The way he said it, I imagine he was rubbing his temples.

"Like what?"

"The questions. You gotta stop with the questions."

"But—"

"No fucking buts, all right? I'll tell you what I think that human brain of yours can comprehend—which, granted, probably won't be much—but the thing is, I'm guiding you through a sort of different reality where the laws of physics and logic as you know them are complete bullshit. Some things, you're just gonna have to see for yourself." He had this way of sounding, not angry, but perpetually annoyed, old and sick of this shit.

As if on cue, the sound of a striking match cut clearly through the void, and the tiniest flicker of light flashed off in the distance. Far off. As far as the stars.

I felt a hand on my shoulder. "There," he said, probably pointing to the light. "See it?"

"The light? Yeah. Only fucking thing I can see."

His hand fell from my shoulder. "Don't get smart. And start walking. That's where we're headed."

I paused to make some mental calculations, tried to determine the distance between us and that flicker, but I had no point of reference. "You're joking, right? Look how far that is. It'll take an eternity to get there."

"Not quite an eternity, there, hot shot."

"But—"

"What did I just say? No buts. Now get moving."

"Seriously, Mr. Bourdain, I just don't see how—"

"You're killin' me, kid." He let out an exaggerated breath. "First off, just call me Tony. This *Mr. Bourdain* bullshit's gonna get old fast. Second, if I tell you it's not that far, and that turns out to be true, will you give it a rest and let me do my job?"

"Sure," I said, knowing full well it would take a lifetime to get to that light. "If it's not that far, I'll stop asking questions. But if it is that far…"

"If it is that far, what will you do, exactly?" Bastard

knew I didn't have any chips to bargain with.

"Oh fuck you." Never meet your heroes, right?

I took a step that seemed to carry me no closer to our destination. I couldn't see Tony or hear his steps, but I could feel that he was still there, walking beside me. That first step had taken me nowhere, but the second could have covered the width of the Pacific, and the third was like stepping over the Milky Way the way children avoid cracks in the sidewalk. I landed the fourth step, and we were there, at a fancy podium lit by a single black candle illuminating a magnificently thick ledger and the thin, worn face of a man. His nose was the shape of a bird of prey's beak, curved to a point over his pencil mustache. His hair was slicked back and black as the void, a vivid contrast to his gleaming white tuxedo with matching shirt and bowtie. He was on the phone—a landline, if you can believe that shit—and had his ear plugged with the index finger of his free hand. He didn't so much as glance up when we appeared.

Tony's smile was beaming victory. "Close enough for you, kid?"

"Holy shit that was awesome!"

"Wild, right?"

"That was like making the jump to light speed or some shit! How are you so calm?"

"You get used to it after a few millennia." He casually pulled a toothpick from a little cup on the podium. "Now, about all those questions."

"Yeah, yeah. I'll keep them to a minimum. But I still wanna know how—"

"Different reality. Ninety percent of the time, the

answer will be different reality."

"Right. And here I thought you were just taking me to a nice restaurant."

"*Nice*," Tony repeated. "*Nice* is, well, a subjective kind of thing."

"Come now, Tony," the maître d' chimed in, hanging up his phone. "We are a very nice place, no?"

Tony nodded. "No offense meant, of course, Pierre. You know this is my favorite spot throughout all the Netherworlds. I tell all my friends."

"Yes, yes," Pierre said, waving his hand at Tony's words like shooing off a fly. "You always say such nice things, Tony. But I still do not understand why you must call me 'Pierre'. You know this is not my name. All this time, it is always Pierre."

"I call all French people Pierre," Tony said. "Just a stupid American joke."

"I am not even French," Pierre said, shaking his head and leaning heavily into his thick French accent. "So many Americans over the years, and I will never understand the humor, but it is good to see you. Why do you come without a reservation?"

Tony, for the first time I noticed, tensed. "Yeah," he said, swiveling his shoulders and head just a little, like dancing around something, "it's sort of a last-minute thing. I thought maybe you could let us through without the wait. You know, a favor for an old friend? I mean, you're not that busy tonight, right?"

"*Tsk*, *tsk*, Tony. You should know better. We are busy every night. Business is, as you Americans would say, exploding."

Tony dropped his toothpick onto the podium and grabbed another. "Of course I know better. You know I wouldn't just pop in like this. The GM is expecting a call from you, actually."

In an instant, Pierre's demeanor totally changed, the snooty Frenchman routine dropped like Tony's spit-soaked toothpick, which Pierre was just now picking up from the top page of the ledger with a white linen and a disgusted sneer. "The GM?"

Tony leaned an elbow onto the podium. "I know it's kinda your thing, keeping people waiting, but you might wanna get on the horn there, Frenchy."

"I see," Pierre said, finally shifting his attention to me, looking me up and down suspiciously. "And who is your...friend?"

Tony looked me over as well before answering. "Yeah, I know. We didn't exactly have time to worry about the dress code."

Instinct got me to look down at my clothes. My shoes were recently polished and slacks recently pressed, I'd washed and ironed my shirt only yesterday, and my tie was straight and tied at the appropriate length. "What's wrong with what I'm wearing?"

Pierre shook his head and plucked the phone off the receiver, *ts*king again and rolling his eyes at Tony. "I leave that to you, old friend," he said, pressing a button on the phone and putting the receiver to his ear.

I straightened my already straight tie. "Seriously? What's wrong?"

Tony inspected my outfit once more. "Well, they're usually pretty strict about the whole dinner jacket bit."

"Why would you even bring me here if I can't get in without a jacket?"

"Don't worry. We'll get around the jacket." He brushed my shoulders off with the back of his hand, then took hold of my tie, pulling it towards him, holding it between his fingers. "I gotta say, though, as much as I enjoy the clever nerdiness of a tie that prominently features a TIE-fighter—and believe me, I do—I'm afraid the sheer gaudiness of it might be a problem for ol' Pierre."

"Well excuse me," I said, leaning back so my TIE tie slid from his hand. "If I'd have known we were going someplace so fancy, I'd have busted out the USS Enterprise." I looked around, but all I could see outside our little lighted spot at the host stand was the void. "Where are we, anyway?"

Tony started to speak to Pierre but was shushed with an index finger long as a fucking mop handle. He responded by reaching into Pierre's podium and searching for something. "Ah, there it is."

I heard a click, then a little whir, and all at once the void lit up and took shape.

Chairs and benches with backs too upright to be comfortable, little ponds along the walls fed by little waterfalls, lined with plastic bamboo shoots and stocked with rainbows of koi—this was obviously some sort of waiting room. And the people. Everywhere, people were milling about, looking at the framed prints of kitchen wares and stills of dessert platters that hung on the walls. Every now and again they'd check their watches and cell phones, cross and uncross their arms, impatiently tap their toes.

At first it seemed like any other waiting room, except for its size. But then I noticed that half of the people were drenched with sweat, removing jackets and rolling up shirtsleeves, fanning themselves with paper takeout menus. The other half were shivering cold, bouncing to get the blood flowing, pulling their arms inside their clothes, breathing steam into cupped hands to warm their fingers.

"You done yet?" It was someone behind us.

I turned to see a man, nondescript from his dull hair to his boring shoes. His nose and cheeks were red and dry, his arms crossed over his chest, rubbing vigorously at his biceps. One of the cold ones, then. I looked at Tony, who looked at Pierre, who was still on the phone, a finger plugging his ear. Tony looked back at me and nodded.

"Uh, yeah. I guess we're done," I said.

"Then how 'bout you get the fuck out of the way so I can talk to twinkle toes, here?" The man threw his chin in Pierre's direction.

Now, I can take that kind of shit from a person who's socially bound to tip me at the end of our interaction, but if I'm not at work, that dough won't rise, you know? But I must still have been in shock about, well, everything. Instead of berating him, I actually fucking apologized and stepped aside to stand next to Tony, who was now pulling the Marlboro Man lean against the wall beside some sort of fake plastic tree.

"Guess I know who'll be wearing the pants in this relationship," he said.

I was about to come back with some sort of cutting and witty remark, but the man began banging his open palm on the ledger. "Hey!" he shouted, "Nancy! Get off the phone! You got a customer here!"

Without looking up, Pierre raised the same finger he had with Tony, meaning, of course, *wait*.

The man sent the ledger and cup of toothpicks off the podium and skidding across the floor. The moment the pages and picks were still, they vanished, only to instantly reappear on the podium. I was still awestruck by this whole materialization thing, but it seemed to have no effect on the man—he just sent the things flying, again and again, until Pierre finally hung up the phone and lowered his finger.

"May I be of service, sir?" Pierre said, throwing in as much snoot as he could, I assume just for the fun of it.

The man lowered his hands to his sides. "Damn right you can be of service," he said, trying, like angry customers often do, to sound authoritative, like Pierre was merely *the help*. "I've been waiting in here entirely too long. This is totally unacceptable."

Pierre *tut-tut*-ed, shook his head apologetically. "I'm so terribly sorry, sir. I will do everything I can to rectify the situation. How long have you been waiting, exactly?"

The man looked at his watch, aggressively tapped its face, then held it to his ear, shaking it, listening for a tick. "Damn thing," he said. "I don't know exactly how long, but just the same it's been too long. Entirely too fucking long."

"As you have said, sir."

"I demand to know when my table will be ready."

"Of course, sir. Please allow me a moment to check the list." Pierre slowly ran his long, bony index finger down column after column, page after page of names, finally stopping and tapping on one, like punctuation. "Ah yes. There we are. Thank you for your considerable patience, sir. Your table will be ready in twenty minutes."

The man turned his attention to Tony and me. "Twenty minutes?! Can you believe that shit?"

Tony, still selling cigarettes, shrugged. "That's about the shortest wait you'll find in this part of town without a reservation. I'd say you're coming out ahead, my friend."

Just like that, the man's anger subsided. He puffed up his chest and adjusted his belt. "Well, when you put it that way, I guess you're right. See, that's why I never bother making a reservation. If the wait's only gonna be twenty minutes, why go through the hassle, amiright? Oh, and Nancy?" he continued, turning back to the unfazed maître d', "get someone to turn the heat up, will ya? It's fucking freezing in here." And off he went to rejoin the others in their waiting.

"Twenty minutes now?" Tony asked Pierre, who was fiddling with an analog thermostat on the wall. "What happened to a half-hour?"

"People happened, Tony. They do not have the patience they once did, so we changed it to twenty."

"Wait," I cut in, immediately seeing the appalled look on Pierre's face, and correcting myself. "*Pardonne moi*. But how long has that guy actually been waiting?"

Pierre and Tony looked at each other and burst out

laughing. Once Pierre was able to steady himself without the aid of the podium and catch his breath, he slammed the ledger closed. "How would I know such a thing?"

"You found his name in the book, and—"

"He has no name here," Pierre answered. "But he thinks he does, so I acted like I was looking for him. Works every time."

"But you said twenty minutes, and—"

"It's always twenty minutes, kid," said Tony, finally forcing himself off the wall. "Well, now it is, anyway. An eternity of waiting twenty more minutes."

I looked out at all those poor souls, trapped in a room together, waiting just to wait. I looked at my watch—the face shaped like the Millennium Falcon because even in the world of geeky men's fashion accessories, continuity is paramount—but the second hand was frozen. I looked at my cell phone, but no service.

"Might as well feed that thing to the slug," Tony said. "Not much use in here."

"The slug?"

"Theirs don't work, either," he said, turning me to see the crowd and avoiding the question about the slug. "But they keep checking, just to make sure. Amazing thing, hope."

Now, I've always considered myself a reasonably intelligent guy, quick on the uptake, able to extrapolate conclusions from incomplete data, but I couldn't wrap my head around any of this. The broken phones and watches, the room appearing out of nowhere, the snarky maître d' with his thermostat and curlicue-corded phone, his apparent disdain for the Star Wars franchise. And speaking of Star Wars, that warp drive thing.

Tony must have noticed my head was about to explode. "If you have questions, and I know you do, now would be the time."

And boy, did I have questions. All the questions. So many questions I couldn't figure out which to ask first, so I just stood there, mouth agape, staring at the crowd.

"All right. I guess we'll just have to lay it out for you. This," he said, waving an arm out in front of me, presenting the room, "is the waiting room."

"Yeah," I said, finally finding my voice. "That much I figured out."

"Good. Not a complete moron, then."

"How long have they been waiting?"

"That's a little trickier to explain," he said. "Time doesn't work the same way here as it does out there. The thing about eternity is it doesn't really have a starting point, or an ending point, for that matter. It just *is*. Follow?"

I nodded, but I might have been lying, just a little. "But if time works differently here, why tell them twenty minutes?"

Tony turned to the maître d'. "Pierre?"

"Ah yes." Pierre looked out over the sea of people. "We tell them twenty minutes because that is the perfect amount of time. Long enough that they know they must wait, yet short enough they are always thinking they will be seated soon. As Tony said, hope is an amazing thing, no?"

"And no one ever just gets sick of waiting and tries

to leave?"

"Some of the time," Pierre continued, "one of them will come to me, like that, ahem, *gentleman* just did, and they will carry on for a moment, demanding to be taken to their table, but there is no way for them to leave, so the thought never enters their brains."

"I don't get it."

"Don't sweat it, kid," Tony said, giving me a pat on the back. "One of those things that tiny brain just can't understand. As far as they know, they are waiting to get into the restaurant, and that's all they'll ever know."

"Okay, so if I'm getting this right, this place is basically Purgatory, yeah?"

"That's pretty much the gist of it. If you're one of those people who perpetually shows up on a Saturday night without a reservation, and then you get all upset about the wait, this is where you end up. An eternity of waiting twenty more minutes, watching others get seated before you."

"I guess that makes sense." I'd been watching the crowd throughout my lesson, and I now noticed that the man who had come up to the host stand no longer rubbed himself for warmth. He had taken off his jacket and was now unbuttoning his shirtsleeves. "So what's the deal with the temperature thing, then? Some people are freezing, some are sweating their asses off, and they're standing right next to each other."

Tony grinned. "Pierre?"

Pierre grinned, too. "When they complain about the heat, I make it cold. When they complain about the cold, I make it hot. Waiting should never be too comfortable a thing, no?"

"But how are they—"

"This is Restaurant Hell, kiddo," Tony said. "Things won't always make sense to you. I know this place better than almost anyone, and things don't even always make sense to me. But torture is what Hells are known for, you know?"

The phone rang. Pierre answered it. "Heard, boss," he said before hanging it up again. "You can take him in now, Tony. But I must warn you, we have been having trouble with the doors. They are being repaired, but until everything is fixed, there is no telling in which dining room you will find yourself."

"Jesus," Tony said. "Even in the only restaurant in Hell, it's always something."

"*Oui*," chortled Pierre. Then, to me, "Due to the circumstances, you do not need to wear a jacket. But if I may..." He reached beneath the podium and came out with an elegant blood-red tie, dangled the thing in front of me. "In the interest of good taste, no?"

Tony laughed. I did not.

I narrowed my eyes at Pierre, and he shrugged his shoulders. "As you wish," he said. He turned around and pulled aside a red velvet curtain that appeared out of fucking nowhere, revealing a set of double doors with pitchfork handles. "Enjoy your experience," he said, smiling and sounding sincere enough.

"Always good to see you, Pierre," Tony said as he gestured me towards the doors.

"*Oui oui*, Tony. You as well." The phone rang again, and Pierre turned back to answer it.

Tony took the handle of the door on the left, and I grabbed the one on the right.

"Um, one more question before we go on?"

"Shoot, kid."

"What's Pierre's real name?"

"I honestly can't remember," Tony said. "But it's been so long it would be rude to ask now."

THREE

We passed through the curtain and the double doors. The curtain was silent as it swung back to the floor, but the closing doors were once again thunderous, the darkness again all-encompassing. I wish I could say having experienced this once already made me more comfortable this second time around, but I'd be lying. True nothingness is terrifying in a way I'll never be able to truly express.

Though I was again monumentally freaked out, I did my best not to let Tony know it. "So," I said, nearly successful in keeping my voice steady, "this happens every time, then?"

"Yep."

I was hoping for a little more than *yep*, but I can't say I was surprised by his curt response. It was plain to see he got a kick out of watching me struggle. Sure, he was working, but that didn't mean he couldn't enjoy it.

The man had to be bored. Thousands of years is a long time.

"We just, what, wait here until something appears?"

"Yep."

I've always been comfortable with silence, but this was too much. So I kept talking. "Must be wild. I mean, all these years guiding people through Hell? You must have met some pretty interesting people."

A grunt, finally, and then, in that condescending tone of his, "Some more interesting than others."

I'd merely been filling the dead space, but it got me thinking. "Like, I can't imagine Hitler was a very good customer."

"Everyone hears Hell, and their first thought is always Hitler. Humans used to be a lot more interesting," Tony said. I expected him to just let me keep rambling in that self-important yet somehow also globally magnanimous way of his, but oh that Tony, he's just full of surprises. "Never met him," he said, "but I've heard he's a surprisingly polite guy, other than that whole master race and genocide thing. Of course, given where we are, it's best to take that kind of thing with a grain of salt."

"Wait. Hitler's not here?"

"Not here. You know that saying *there's a special kind of Hell for people like you*? Well, he's in a very special Hell."

Even given the cliché, I'd never imagined there could really be more than one Hell. But, now that he'd said it, it made sense.

"How many Hells are there?"

"More than I'll ever see," he said. "I'll never die, and I'll still never see them all."

"Damn. An eternity of Hells. No wonder you're so cranky."

He didn't have time to respond, if he even wanted to, because out of the darkness came a click and a thin fizzle of electricity, a whir that immediately morphed into "Margaritaville" by Jimmy Buffet, but at a volume wholly unfit for such a relaxed jam. I covered my ears just as the lights flashed on, as bright as the music was loud. All kinds of light: exposed track lights with clean white bulbs; beer signs, hideous neons of all colors, as though a rainbow had been ripped to shreds and had its innards retwisted into monstrous gaud; strings of white Christmas lights; even tiki torches dotted the room, their tiny flames like diamond buttons on a platinum-spun suit, sparks of unapologetic excess.

Amidst all this brightness was an explosion of kitsch. In one corner, a man-sized wooden carving of a bear had a beer bottle strapped to one of its paws, a lacy pink bra dangling from the claws on the other. The ceiling was all shimmering plastic pennants, festive Corona and Bud Light Lime banners announcing that Summer has arrived, and that means it's time for lots of crap-ass suds. On the walls: posters of scantily clad blondes arched seductively over the hoods of sports cars; trash-can-lid-sized logos of seemingly every sports team that has ever competed anywhere on the planet; and novelty crap including but not limited to those fish that sing "Don't Worry Be Happy" when you wander unfortunately close to their motion sensors.

It was a barrage on the senses.

My hands still muffling my ears, my eyes slits like

back when I first started smoking pot, I looked over at Tony, and even he seemed to be reeling a little from the bombardment. He wasn't shielding himself from it like I was, but he looked tense, more so than usual, like every muscle in his body was going rigid to withstand the attack.

"What is this place?" I shouted, but by the way he shrugged his shoulders and shook his head, I knew he couldn't hear me. I couldn't even hear myself over this wretched din.

I took a crunchy and sticky step towards him, the floor covered in spent peanut shells and pools of drying beer, but he raised a hand to stop me and pointed at the floor, where a series of hoses snaked their way through the shells and swamp of spilt swill. They tangled on and through themselves, in some places looping up in a way that could easily ensnare a wandering and bewildered foot such as my own.

Standing still, ears still covered, eyes still asquint, I followed the hoses. They slithered around the feet of the barstools and climbed like vines up over the neon lights of the bar, which I could now see was an island. At each corner of the island stood a fountain, those chocolate fountain deals you see at weddings. One of them looked like it may have actually been flowing with chocolate, but I had no way of really knowing. Judging by the colors of the stuff flowing in the other three, I guessed nacho cheese, ranch dressing, and maybe some monstrous blend of the two.

The hoses dipped behind the bar and rose again to the island within the island, that place where one would expect to find the booze. But nary a bottle was to be found.

Atop this middle island sprawled a gelatinous mass, a slimy monstrosity of a thing, somehow much larger than should have been possible given the size of the room. Jabba the Hutt instantly sprung to mind. Unlike Jabba, though, this thing appeared to be covered with thousands upon thousands of teats, each connected to its own hose. After considerable searching, I finally located what I thought might be the end with the head. My guess was informed mainly by how the folds of flesh appeared to be grinning with an obscene amount of pleasure, but it also had something to do with the friendly neighborhood grandmother hairdo, perfectly coiffed and an elegant silver.

I didn't vomit so much as bile and bits of whatever I'd last eaten bubbled out of me, running down my chin and my TIE tie, eventually to pool in my left shoe and mingle with the other foulness on the floor.

Before I could get a wrist up to wipe my chin, a black linen found its way to my lips and gently soaked up the mess. Holding the linen was a hand with over-stuffed sausage fingers and chipped pastel-pink nail polish. Connected to the hand was more of a tentacle than an arm, and the tentacle was connected to someplace on the slug I could not see.

I tried to turn my head to find Tony, but those greasy fingers caught me by the chin and held firm, giving the monster time to maneuver itself into a more tenable position for eye contact. Not that it softened the hideousness in any way, but the beast had surprisingly warm, friendly eyes.

"There, there, dear," it said, voice soft and nurturing, almost sing-song-y with its Georgia accent, somehow soothing even when loud enough to be heard over the music and mélange of other restaurant sounds. "No need to be embarrassed. You're hardly the first person to have, shall we say, released themselves on our floor. And honey, I reckon you won't be the last."

My mouth tasted like the other side of a fried pickle, and my stomach was threatening to give me another taste. I've never been more repulsed by a thing in my life, and I never will be again, but I wasn't the least bit afraid. I was, in fact, oddly comforted.

It smiled at me, I think. "I know just the thing to fix you up. Don't you worry, sweetheart. Before you know it, you'll be right as rain."

I could have fallen asleep inside that voice, and it almost felt as though I had.

"Now," it continued, "Everything is better when it's a surprise. Close your eyes and try to remember the best feeling you ever felt. Not what gave you the feeling, but the feeling itself. And when you open your eyes, you'll be amazed by what I have for you."

I knew I shouldn't, but its voice made me want to. I closed my eyes and sifted through feelings until I was lost in them, until I could sense… something. Something like the scent of a warm breakfast in a cabin by a lake in winter. Something like laughter. Something like a full sack at the end of a successful Halloween night.

"Open 'em up, darlin'," it said, voice like a slow sunrise.

I opened my eyes to find a second sausage-tentacle hand, a gleaming white serviette resting on its open palm. Resting on the serviette, a maple bacon doughnut glistening with syrup and pig fat, perfectly golden, so light and airy I didn't need to hold it or eat it to know.

The smile again, maybe. "Doesn't that look just wonderful?"

It was all I could do to nod.

"No point in just letting it sit there lookin' pretty, is there? Here," and the doughnut was brought to my lips, "have a bite."

It's difficult to describe the sensation of this doughnut without sounding at best hyperbolic, or at worst like a man with a doughnut fetish. The moment that first bite hit my tongue, my consciousness was expelled from my body like it wouldn't survive the flavor explosion intact and was ejected for its own protection.

From this vantage point, hovering in a massless state a few feet above my body, I could see what was really going on here.

First, my body—there I was, held upright by one pulsating tentacle while another crammed a lump of glistening white goop into my mouth. I was grinning like an imbecile, eyes rolled back in my head from the sheer bliss of this certainly not a maple bacon doughnut. Stupid things, bodies.

Then there was Tony, off to my left, struggling to free himself from yet another tentacle while shouting words not even my ephemeral form could comprehend through the noise.

Then there was the noise, which I noticed now was

not simply over-played party songs turned up to eleven, but also the constant deep and loud hum of some sort of machine, and the perpetual and unmistakable gaseous releases of fellow human beings.

I found the source of the flatulence first. As I turned my attention from the island bar and the gross slug thing to the rest of the room, I saw them: endless rows of armchairs, each with a person sitting in it, each person continually cramming food into their mouth. The only other movement I detected from them was the occasional subtle lift of a leg, the telltale sign of letting one rip. And it wasn't just gas. They were sitting in their own runny, stinking feces, adding to the mess with each shift of an ass cheek. Every man and woman in the place—there were, again, no children—looked equal parts delighted and disgusted.

The food on their plates—the same white goop as my supposed doughnut—was perpetually replenished by the tubes that ran along the floor. I followed the tubes and found that they were connected to a machine on the ceiling, which was in turn connected to all the hoses sucking on the Hutt's teats.

"There, there, dear," the monster went on. "See? I knew that was what you needed. And what goes better with a fresh, warm, maple bacon doughnut than a nice big swig of cold milk?" Yet another tentacle was approaching my body, this one carrying one of the same hoses pumping all those poor saps with god knows what. The thing was dripping, or more like oozing, from the tip. If I'd been in my body, I'd have puked again.

Having no idea how I was booted out of my body,

I also had no idea how to get back in. My consciousness, though very much in working order, was still reliant on my meatsuit for certain basic needs—namely, at the moment, motor functions. Swim as I might, I could only flail in the air.

Even while flailing, I could still hear. The only reason I noticed was that I could suddenly hear Tony. Clearly. "Don't let her stick that thing in your mouth, you dumb shit! I swear to fucking Christ, I'll never let you live it down!" He was charging full steam, those long lanky legs leaping over barstools and toppled tray-stands, his cowboy boots obliterating the stale peanut shells, grinding them to dust on the floor. As he ran and shouted, he held a lit tiki torch before him like a flaming short-spear. Valiant, for the specter of a chef.

The slug whipped at him with yet another tentacle, but he caught it with the flame just before it got to him. The slug roared—a sound decidedly unlike that soothing grandmother voice from a minute ago—and I was pulled violently back into my body. Luckily for me, it appears one's consciousness cannot get whiplash, at least not in the physical sense.

Just as that stupid grin fell from my face, Tony came barreling into my side, knocking me down and out of the slug's grasp. The body can always get whiplash.

"Up, now," Tony said, panting, pointing to a door beyond the bar. "Run. And don't fucking eat anything."

When someone guides you through Hell, and they tell you to run, common sense dictates it wise to do so. So I got up and fucking booked it, man. I hooked the nacho cheese fountain to help me take the first corner, somehow managed to avoid the snags of hoses and catch the ranch fountain to round the last corner, and bounded for home. I flat-out dove through the doors, light on their hinges, great for me but not for Tony. They swung back quickly and stopped him something like dead.

As though from a great distance I heard him say, "You motherf—," and then nothing.

No sounds other than my own breath and beating heart. No light. The only tactile feeling the bile seeping into my socks. The only smell the smell of me, left arm dripping nacho cheese and ranch, TIE tie heavy with stomach juices. And I also may have pooped myself.

FOUR

I stood there, my left arm dripping a mucousy white substance that stunk from Hell to high Heaven, my left foot sloshing around inside my shoe in a foulness of my own creation. My head spun in the darkness. I couldn't tell if I was breathing. I was a fucking mess, and I was alone.

Alone and in the void, but the void was different this time. Or maybe it wasn't the void that was different, but my state of mind. After what I'd just experienced, complete and utter nothingness was a welcomed escape. As a life-long food service professional, I don't really have much experience with vacations, but this was easily in my top two.

So good, this respite, that I was devastated to hear that match-strike, see that dot of flame out in the black. Worse, it wasn't far off like before, but was only about six feet in front of me, and I could already see that snooty sneer Pierre wore as naturally as he did that stereotypically French mustache.

He sniffed the air before looking up from his ledger, locating the source of the stench. Upon seeing me he tilted his head up and turned his face to the side, unsubtly, an obvious attempt to get as far from my stink as possible, an easy way to show his disgust at me being here in the first place.

"Ah, yes," he said as I stooped in panic, defeat, and other, fouler things. "I see you've experienced our Gluttony Room. I do hope you found everything to your liking."

I continued my silent immobility, the feeling of that ooze sliding from my fingers dominating my thoughts and my body. Wretched as it was, had I been able to summon the strength to raise my arm, I'd have sucked those fingers fucking dry.

Pierre reached into his podium and pulled out a gleaming, pressed white linen. He was meticulous about pinching the last thread of the corner, allowing the thing to unfurl before leaning back as far as he could and holding it out for me.

"May I recommend, sir, that you tend to yourself," he said, waving the linen to get my attention. "I'm afraid our other guests may find your current state a touch, shall we say, off-putting."

I glared at him and found the strength to grab the linen and commence sopping. Speech, however, still escaped me.

Pierre immediately reached for a second linen. "No complaints? Wonderful. Management will be pleased to know it."

He handed me the fresh linen just as I dropped the first to the floor with a sickening slap. Now that I was somewhat back into myself, I looked at the goop that remained on my hand and without a moment's hesitation raised that hand to my mouth, index and middle fingers extended.

"Ah, ah, ah," Pierre said, like wagging that freakishly long finger in my face. "May I also recommend that you do not do what it appears you are about to do, by which I of course mean lick the, ahem, *milk* from your fingers. I do understand the temptation, of course. The employees here at The Inferno sample all the food and beverages so we are better able to treat our guests."

"You mean better able to *mistreat* your guests, don't you?" I said, staring at my glistening fingertips, still tantalizingly close to my lips.

He laughed, but it was more like mimicking laughter. "Indeed, sir."

I could have punched him, but now that I'd found my voice I'd also rediscovered my instinct for self-preservation. "What is this shit?" I asked, still eying my fingers.

"It is everything," he said like he thought I should have known this already. "Everything you have ever wanted and everything you might ever want. An eternity of gratification. Unending, unrelenting pleasure. All there, on the tips of your fingers."

I looked suspiciously at my goopy hand and then narrowed my eyes at Pierre. "Well that doesn't sound very Hellish."

"He neglected to tell you that it's also the excrement of an ancient and incredibly unholy beast of the underworld that survives off two things, the feeling of instant gratification and the gases emitted by human excrement. A sort of endless poop-loop." Tony had apparently materialized as I was getting a hard-on for the goop.

I dropped my hand to my side and spun to see him—or, at the very least, the tall, slender shape of him. Whereas I had managed to escape with only my arm coated in demonic slug poo, Tony had not been so lucky. He looked like a Krispy Kreme doughnut that had been forgotten on the dashboard of a locked car on a sunny summer afternoon, withered and slimy with glistening melted glaze. His designer button-down and sports jacket had been replaced by the lacy pink bra from the claws of the wooden grizzly. His cowboy boots were also gone, exposing long, slimy toes and one motherfucker of an ingrown toenail.

"Yes, yes," Pierre said, seemingly unfazed by the sight of a soiled Tony. "Pleasure, excrement. Excrement, pleasure. In the end it is all the same, no?"

"Holy shit, Tony," I said, looking for one of the waiting room's koi ponds to wring out my oversaturated linen. "Man, I'm so sorry. I didn't realize the doors would... and the, you know, the void and everything." I held the wet linen out for him, but he didn't take it. "How did you get out?"

Pierre snorted, and when Tony and I turned on him with judgmental eyes, not one lip hair twitched.

"Zip it, Frenchie," Tony said.

Pierre lowered his gaze in a sort of half-bow. "I am so sorry, Tony," he said, tossing another linen our way, where Tony snatched it out of the air like proving a point. "I did not mean to interrupt. If you would be so kind as to regale us with the undoubtedly harrowing tale of your escape? And please, spare no detail."

Tony wiped his face and chucked the linen back to/at Pierre, who dodged skillfully with a grin, the linen landing on the floor behind him. Pierre then nodded once and opened his hands, both actions like expectations, like saying, *Come on, then. Out with it.*

Tony took a deep breath, closed his eyes, and went red. I can't be sure, but it felt to me that his cheeks flushed not with anger, as I'd have expected, but with shame. "Even I don't need to know the details," he said, maybe to Pierre and me, maybe to himself. "But hey, I've done worse."

I was close enough to smell the slime on him, and it far overpowered the slime on me. I'd have licked him clean, all that tempting goo just begging to be inside me, but the aroma of something else stopped me. I've smelled fear, shame, and pain before, but not like this. I raised my dry hand and motioned for Pierre to toss another linen. To my surprise, the maître 'd was quick with it. I caught it and moved to clean up my guide, but Tony caught me by the wrist.

"Don't even fucking think about it, kid," he said, yanking the linen from my hand. "I think you've done enough."

"Come on, man. Don't be like that. I didn't know. You told me to run, so I ran, you know?" For the record,

I really was sorry.

"Yeah, yeah. Save it." He took off the bra, spilling two C-cups worth of demonic excrement to the floor. "I know, all right? Just…give me a minute. I fucking hate dealing with that thing. Only thing that's ever managed to make me feel dirty." He shivered like he'd never before felt the cold.

I looked again at my own hand. "What, uh, what was that thing anyway?"

Tony said nothing as he used the linen to rid his skin of some of the mucous and without a glance raised a finger to shush me.

Pierre cleared his throat. "That was the Glutton," he said, looking to Tony for permission to continue, which was granted by a slight nod of the head. "Though it prefers to be called Paulina. A Guardian of Hell, ancient, and one of the most powerful. As Tony said, it feeds off the feeling of instant gratification, which you silly humans seem unable to resist. Take your fingers away from your mouth."

I hadn't realized I'd even lifted my hand, but back down it went.

"Its…*secretions*, shall we say…influence the mind of the sinner when imbibed. Which is to say, of course, that the sinner is tricked into believing they are in Heaven, receiving all they ever could have wanted. In some fashion, at least."

He tossed another linen to Tony, who continued the explanation. "To them, it's all ice cream and never-ending shrimp at Red fucking Lobster, and they just sit there, stuffing their faces, unable to stop themselves."

"Still doesn't sound all that bad," I said, dwelling on exactly how delicious that maple bacon doughnut was, even if it was only a doughnut in my head. "I mean, what kind of punishment is that, really? Even if you're only being tricked into believing you get everything you want, you still think you're getting everything you want, right? Sounds to me like they're gaming the system."

Pierre chortled at that. "I am afraid, Tony, that your young friend may never understand," he said, readying himself to toss another linen to his other-dimensional coworker.

Tony, however, waved off the napkin. "That should be enough, Pierre. And I'm afraid of that, too, but he is my charge, and none of your concern."

Pierre again bowed his head.

Tony turned his attention back to me. "You might think that," he said, "but what goes in one end has to come out the other, right? Some of those people have been shitting themselves pretty much nonstop for decades. They sit there, unable to stop themselves from eating no matter how full they feel, shitting all over themselves and all over each other, while the Glutton is just plopped there, covered in teats and tubes, moaning like it's in the throes of perpetual orgasm." He shivered again. "Man that thing's gross."

I gagged a little, but it didn't seem that either Tony or Pierre noticed. "Okay then," I said, swallowing hard, trying not to let myself vomit again. "Hell."

"It serves them right, no?," Pierre chimed in. "Fingers. Down."

I lowered my hand again. "Why do I keep doing

that?"

"You can't help it," Tony said, slicking his hair back, shaking the excess goop from his hands. "That stuff's irresistible to humans. It's what makes Paulina such an effective Guardian."

I couldn't argue with that. If what they'd been saying hadn't seemed so important, I wouldn't have heard a word, driven as I was to get that shit on my tongue. "What happens if I, you know…?"

Pierre nestled a yellow #2 pencil between his fingers, where, although the pencil was brand new, it looked like one of those tiny things they give you on a miniature golf course. He made ready to write. "Shall I pencil you in for an eternal reservation?"

"Ah. I see. Um, no, thank you." I'd have chewed off my hand to quell the temptation, but the goop still would have gotten into my mouth. "Who are the sinners?"

Tony reached around the podium and fumbled around for a moment. There was a click, and out of the void materialized a door. He opened it to expose a closet full of expensive-looking suits, ties, jackets, slacks, and, of course, cowboy boots. "You've been in this business a long time," he said, running his fingers over the fabrics. "Who do you think?"

I didn't really even need to ask in the first place. "People who ask for extra ranch for, well, anything, really," I said. "Anyone who eats at Golden Corral or Cracker Barrel. People who tell the bartender to make it strong but get pissed when there's an upcharge for a double. People who stash rolls or sugar packets in their pockets and purses. People who go to an all-you-can-eat-buffet, eat plate after plate, and then get upset when there's a no-take-out policy. People who drink enough free refills of Diet Coke to fill an Olympic-sized swimming pool." I stopped only because I was out of breath. "That about right?"

Tony looked at Pierre, who pursed his lips and nodded in a way that suggested defeat, like he'd just lost a bet. "Not bad," Pierre said, turning to me, "for a human. But there is more. Much more. You have neglected those who—"

"I think the kid's got the gist of it, Pierre," Tony said as he slid into a new jacket, identical to the one he'd lost escaping the Glutton. "Now, if you don't mind, I'd like to get as far from that abomination as possible, and we have a reservation to keep."

Pierre nodded, but not before huffing and rolling his eyes. "Of course, Tony."

"Wait a minute," I said.

"Christ," Tony grunted. "What now?"

I looked down at my own soiled attire, and Tony got the point. "Pierre, open the kid's closet."

Pierre found some other button under his podium, and another door appeared and opened. The options were nowhere near as classy as Tony's, but they were dry. I chose all black because it seemed fitting, and I might even be able to keep it at least appearing to be clean. None of the ties spoke to me, though, so after wringing it out in a koi pond I hadn't already contaminated, I tied the TIE tie back under my collar.

Tony shook his head at me. "Really?"

He looked to Pierre. "I tried," said the Frenchman.

"If this were Fashion Hell, your young friend would indeed be doomed."

I sighed. "Yeah, yeah. You don't like my tie. Whatever. Think maybe one of you can tell me where we're off to next?"

The specters looked at each other but said nothing.

"Well? If you give me fair warning, maybe this time I'll be able to get out without fucking you over again."

Still, nothing.

"Tony," I said, knowing full well that Pierre would be of no help to me, "where are we going next?"

Pierre was already on the phone, supposedly busy, and searching with a blind hand for whichever button would take us to our next dining experience. He pressed it, and the red curtains again appeared, Tony taking a step towards them.

"I don't know, exactly," he said, buttoning the top two buttons on his new three-button jacket, "but it's nowhere I haven't been before."

FIVE

The heavy slam of an invisible door and then nothing. Tony was right—already this was beginning to feel, not exactly normal, but at least less terrifying. There was apparently nothing to worry about in the void itself, it was what would appear out of it that was the problem. I was fully aware that my tiny little human brain couldn't even imagine whatever horrors awaited us out there in the black, and that was what scared me most.

It seemed this rift thing typically took a minute or two, though, so at least I'd have a little time to gather my—

A click and a whir and up came the lights, though not by much. Even knowing where I was, I found the lighting romantic: electric candelabras on the walls, styled after those carried by young girls in long nightgowns searching a haunted castle, the filaments inside their tall, slender bulbs flickering low watts like candles; real candles, with flames and short wicks, burning on each of the innumerable two-tops; fireplaces evenly spaced around the room, coals glowing while flames gently licked the logs above them.

Warm music—a string quartet, maybe, though I could see neither musician nor P.A. system—hung on the air, slow and understatedly sexy.

From first appearances, this would have been a great place to bring a date.

It was too dark to see much more than the dim outlines of the light fixtures and candles, the vaguely human shapes of people in their seats, but I could sense something in the air. Something sweet. Dessert breads baking in the oven mingled with the faintest wisp of lilac or some other highly aromatic flower. And this might sound a little weird, but I could have sworn I smelled sweat, too. Not body odor sweat, but clean sweat. That fucking-just-after-a-shower kind of sweat, also sweet, but somehow raw, carnal. It was…exciting, somehow. I had to shift in my pants.

I breathed it in deep and held it, exhaled with a little shudder. "Damn."

Tony held his whiff longer than I had. "Right?" he finally said. "Just wait 'til you get a look at her."

"A look at who?"

"That smell's gotta be coming from somewhere, right?"

I sniffed the air again, like for a moment I thought I was a fucking bloodhound. "It's a person that smells like that?"

Tony took another deep breath and spoke as he held it in his lungs. "Not a person. She's definitely something, though." He backhanded my arm to make sure I was paying attention. "Now listen up because this is important. I need you to remember two things right now, kid."

"Okay."

"One, don't fucking eat anything. Or drink anything. In fact, if you have to open your mouth for any reason, cover that shit with your hand. And if anything gets on your hand, for the love of all things unholy, don't lick it off."

"Nothing in the mouth. Got it."

"Good." He rested a hand almost paternally on my shoulder. "Two, when you see how beautiful she is, remember, no matter how Aphrodite-esque the woman, or how Adonis-like the man, somebody somewhere is sick of their shit."

I considered it for a moment. "Wow. I wish I'd have heard that years ago. Would have saved me a lot of trouble."

"Yeah. We've all been there."

"Seriously," I said, pressing the issue because I thought it might help him forgive me for the incident with the Glutton. Flattery will get you everywhere and whatnot. "That's maybe the best advice I've ever heard."

"All right that's enough," Tony said with a roll of his eyes. "You're forgiven for the thing with the slug, all right? Let's just get through this."

"Fine with me. Where are we?"

"This would be Lust. Thought you'd have picked up on that from the, uh, smell," he said, glancing down at my crotch.

I reached down and adjusted myself. "Guess I should have figured."

He laughed. "Don't worry about it, kid. We all get a little weirded out the first time we get a hard-on down here. It'd be kind of fucked up if you didn't, actually."

"Well," I said, finally settled inside my new pants, "good to know I'm relatively normal, I guess."

"Yeah," Tony chuckled. "Relatively."

I ignored that little zinger. "So who are the sinners here, then? I mean, I'm sure I could venture a guess, but…"

Tony took a moment to answer. It was too dark to see him clearly, but I think he was scoping out the room. "We have time, I think," he said. "Go find out."

I looked around, for some reason slightly panicked. "What? You mean just—"

"You've been in this business your whole life. Suddenly afraid to do a little table touch?"

Now, I wouldn't say I was afraid, necessarily, but this was not your typical *hello folks I hope you're enjoying everything thanks for coming out and please come again it was truly a pleasure to serve you* kind of table touch, you know?

"It's not like I can just roll up and be like, Hey guys. How's it going? What are you in for?"

"It's exactly like that, actually," Tony said like he was bored. "They might be sinners, but they're still people. You know how willing people are to talk about themselves."

"Um, okay…"

"Jesus. Just go already. You'll see. I'll grab you if we need to go." Before I could take a step, he grabbed me by both shoulders and looked me in the eye. "But remember—"

"Yeah, yeah. Nothing in the mouth, and somebody somewhere is sick of her shit."

"Right." A shake of my shoulders and he spun me around to face the endless rows of deuces. "Go get 'em, champ."

I took a breath, eyed up a couple sitting four or five tables down, and found myself standing over them. It felt strange. I actually missed having an apron, pen, and notepad—that shit can be like armor. "Hey, guys. How's it going?"

Nothing.

"Enjoying everything so far?"

Still nothing. They just sat there, silently gazing at each other.

"AHEM!!!"

The woman on the banquette to my right finally chirped up. "Oh my god we're so sorry! We just get so lost in each other's eyes sometimes, we forget anything else even exists. Isn't that right, my big strong man?"

From his chair across the table, her big strong man answered, "You know it is, baby."

This was going to be painful, and probably a little gross. But, even without my armor, I was starting to feel more comfortable here, standing over a couple of lovesick morons as they gazed, oblivious to the world around them, into each other's eyes. I'd worked enough Valentine's Days to know how to handle this by now, and at least it was too dark for me to see them make googly eyes or blow kisses or whatever.

I put on my best server voice. "I'm glad to hear you're enjoying yourselves. Where you folks from? You don't sound like locals."

"We're not," he said. "We came in from Toledo. But that's not where we'll be forever, right babe?"

She started bouncing in her seat. "Right, baby. Soon we'll have enough for that house in Columbus, and you'll get that job at the community college, and I'll have my Etsy cookbook chapbook business up and running, and everything will be even more perfect than it already is."

She paused and reached out a hand for her lover, who also reached for her. The moment their fingers touched, the tiny flame shot, no longer so tiny, from the candle. It scorched not only their extended hands but also their faces, which I could now see all too clearly. If he *had* ever been an Adonis, and she an Aphrodite, that point had long since passed. Both were now horribly scarred. The only hair they had left was on the backs of their heads. They didn't even look like people, really—more like cracklins with eyes, all curled and crinkled skin, seared at all the edges.

They pulled away from one another, leaning back to escape the fire, and as the flame died back down I noticed a small plate with two cookies of some sort, covered in a thick layer of dust. I covered my mouth.

"Nobody has ever been more in love than we are," the woman went on, as though she barely noticed getting more of her face burned off. "That's why we're here for free, isn't it, lover?"

"You know it is, baby."

I was still a bit shaken by that sudden spurt of flame,

but they were so enamored with each other they didn't notice how long it took me to finally ask, "Free? How'd you swing that? I mean, this is a pretty swanky place."

The woman started bouncing again, this time adding applause for good measure. "Ooh! Show him the invitation, darling!"

"Already on it, my sweet." He reached inside his dinner jacket and handed me the invite.

I held it up to the fixture on the wall and read it aloud. "We at The Inferno invite you to be our guests for an evening that will feel like an eternity with the only person you want to spend eternity with. All expenses paid for lovers of your singular quality."

"It's a beautiful recognition of our love," she cooed. "Isn't it, my beautiful man?"

"You know it is, baby."

I could have puked right there on the table. Instead, I flipped the invite around to read the back. At first it appeared to be blank, but after a moment, fiery words appeared, like this was the One Invitation to rule them all:

Recipients of this invitation have been proven to have participated in one or more* of the following actions: sitting on the same side of a table when they are the only two guests seated at said table; participating in the extended exchange of bodily fluids via the method of "making out" while at the table or bar; stimulating, via the hand or any other available body part, the erogenous zones of themselves and/or their partners while in the confines of a restaurant or bar setting; ignoring those whose job it is to serve them while getting "lost in each other's eyes".

For a full list of possible transgressions, contact the maître d' at extension 666-69.

The man extended a crispy hand, requesting I return the invitation to him. "What are you looking at?" he asked. "There's nothing on the back."

They couldn't see the fine print, then. Not that they'd have read it anyway.

I handed the thing back to him. "Lemme guess. Handjobs under the table?"

Again the woman bounced and clapped, a lovesick little seal. "Oh my god, baby!!! He knew!" Then, to me, "How did you know? It's his favorite!"

"Just a hunch," I said. But it was more than a hunch. This was a straight-up profiling, and Front of House people excel at profiling. It was plain to see these two were in love, but her giddiness about it compared to his aloofness led me to believe that she felt the need to please him, always, for fear of losing him. A quick handy in public will do the trick every time. "Guess that won't be happening here, though, huh bud?"

The man sighed. "We keep trying, but the table's too damn big."

"At least it's not as disappointing as when the candle stops us from trying to kiss," said the woman. After an uncomfortable moment without a response, she prompted him. "Right, my darling?"

"Oh," he said at last, rolling his eyes, I think—difficult to tell since his eyelids had been burned off long ago. "Right. So much less disappointing than not being able to kiss you, my love."

"Yeah, well good luck with that house in Columbus," I said, already turning on my heel. "And enjoy the rest of your experience here at The Inferno."

I didn't wait for a response. I'd gotten everything I needed. Besides, it wasn't like they were going to tip me—this was an all-expenses-paid dining experience, after all.

Then that smell again, that sense, that tightening of my pants. And then, as out of nothing, and illuminated somehow by something other than light, a pair of giant green eyes, warm and inviting and enticing. What some would call *fuck me eyes*. Below the eyes a cute button nose. Below the cute button nose an enormous smile, plump lips in a port wine shade perfectly framing perfectly straight, white teeth. Below the smile an unobtrusively pointed chin. Below the chin a long, smooth neck. Below the neck acres of creamy soft skin bottlenecking to a valley of cleavage created/exposed by the lowest-cut blouse I've ever seen.

"Oh," almost-whispered the beautiful apparition. "And who might you be?"

Now, I've been with some beautiful women in my time, and I grew up in the era of true supermodels—Cindy Crawford, Elle MacPherson, Naomi Campbell—but this was an entirely new level of sexy. Even the way she asked *and who might you be?* was playful and deadly, more seductive than anything any woman had ever said to me.

It was all I could do to stand there, chin on the floor, lolling tongue like in an old Warner Brothers cartoon, and not crumble to the floor.

"Oh, honey," she said, raising a palm, soft as the scent of a rose, to my cheek. "I didn't mean to frighten you. Here." Her other hand produced a chocolate-covered strawberry, seemingly out of nowhere, and held it tantalizingly close to my lips. "Maybe something sweet will help calm you down."

I stammered, fully aware that the strawberry was probably not a strawberry at all, but still unable to cover my mouth as per Tony's instructions.

"Oh look, you can't even raise your arms. That's adorable." She batted her eyelids, just once, slowly. "Tell you what. I'll help. You open your mouth just a little bit more, and I'll feed it to you. It'll be…fun."

I was trembling all over, except in my pants, where I was throbbing dangerously close to pain. But I didn't open my mouth any wider. I wish I could tell you it was because I was resisting her wiles with everything I had, but in truth I was paralyzed, my heart pumping so much blood that my circulatory system became like a second skeleton, rigid and immovable.

Palm still on my cheek, she slid her thumb gently over my bottom lip. "Come on, gorgeous. It's just a strawberry. Organic. Picked at the height of the season. And the chocolate? Cultivated by the most respected cocoa farmers in all South America. You wouldn't believe what it costs by the pound. Ground it myself, too, and not to brag, but I *really* know my way around a mortar and pestle. Now open up. I promise you won't regret it." Another bat of the eyes. "I'll even let you lick the melted chocolate from my fingertips."

"Drop the strawberry, Gia." It was Tony, and just

in time. "And for fuck's sake stop looking at the kid like that. You got him so riled up his dick's gonna explode like an overstuffed eclair."

"Shit," she said, dropping the fruit. "Tony. I should have known. This one isn't a sinner." She looked me up and down, got her nose close to my neck, and took a long, slow whiff. "Well, not like the rest of these pathetic morons, anyway."

"You're right. He's not. He's with me."

She leaned in and took a whiff of Tony, too. "Damn right he is. Isn't he lucky? Pity, though. It's been ages since I've had a fresh one. How many centuries has it been now, you lanky piece of lovin'?" She ran a finger down the length of his jaw.

He slapped her hand away. "I stopped counting in centuries centuries ago, you skanky piece of hag."

She looked to the floor, but I could tell it wasn't out of shame or defeat. She was trying to play him, manipulate him to some end I'll probably never know. "Don't be like that, Tony. After all this time, I still think about it. About you. You can't tell me you don't think about me, too."

"Oh, you cross my mind from time to time, but I doubt we think about each other the same way."

"Shame," she said, taking hold of my tie and running it slowly between her fingers while slightly nibbling at her bottom lip. "But hopefully there's someone in my future."

She raised her hand to my face again, but Tony caught her by the wrist. "Easy, Gia. He's here with me because the GM wants him here with me."

She wrested her arm free. "Ugh. Fine. He's not ready for me, anyway."

And just like that I regained control of my motor functions, like she'd released me. The hard-on, well, that was going to take a few minutes.

"Holy fuck," I said. Admittedly not my most profound of statements.

"I tried to warn you, kid."

I shook my head like a dog waking from a nap, spittle flying and everything. "I know, but I mean, come on." I looked her up and down with my eyes and, for Tony's benefit, my hand. "No warning can prepare any man for, well, that."

"He's like you, Tony," she said. "Sweet, but not too bright."

"Hey," I said, not knowing what I would say after. "I...uh...fuck you, lady."

Tony lowered and shook his head, pinched the bridge of his nose. "Yeah," he said. "Not too bright. Can't argue with that."

"Fuck off, Tony," I said, realizing I'd again opened my mouth without first covering it with my hand. "This shit isn't my fault. *Go talk to them. We have time. I'll grab you.* You were supposed to have my back. This is on you, you cranky old fuck." Then I thought about it for a second. "Where were you, anyway?"

It was Tony's turn to lower his eyes. "You're right," he said. "I wasn't where I should have been. But I'm here now, and everything's fine. Let's remember that, all right?"

Yeah, I was pissed, but he had a point. He'd saved

me twice now, and I'd be lost if went on without him. So I bowed my head in that way that's meant to convey *yes, I'll acknowledge that we both understand so that you don't have to acknowledge it yourself.*

"That *is* an interesting question," Gia said as she produced another chocolate-covered strawberry from thin air, tonguing just the tip before popping the whole thing in her mouth, then sucking the crumbs of chocolate and strawberry juice from her fingertips. She looked at him, the smirk on her lips long and curved as the California coastline. "Where were you, my sweet?"

Tony sighed. "I was…looking…for something."

"Oh? What would that be?"

"You're really gonna make me say it, aren't you?"

"Oh, honey. You know I am."

He turned to me. "Cover your ears, kid."

"Yeah. No fucking way."

She again traced his jaw, this time with her breath and in the opposite direction, all the way up to his ear. "What were you looking for, Tony?"

He sighed like forcing every last molecule of air from a bellows, shut his eyes, and turned his face to the floor. Then, he went off. "Your fucking macaroons, okay!? It's been at least a thousand years since I've had one of those things. I dream about them. Fucking hell," he said, collapsing to his knees. "I haven't slept since before they built the pyramids, and somehow I still fucking dream about those goddamn macaroons! The crust alone…it's a revelation. That moment you…I mean," his voice shaking now, "you can feel it, hear it, smell it, and taste it all at once. Then that warm, soft dough underneath. Like, fuck, like biting into the upper thigh of a demon who could easily devour your soul," looking up into those green anime eyes, "but instead moans with pleasure and encourages you to move on, let that volcano of sweet creamy filling form islands of life on that long-barren tongue, almost as old as the oceans."

I swear to everything I've ever thought holy, Tony was fucking weeping, soaking up snot and tears with his starched cuffs. And the way he talked about the macaroons, so soft and poetic.

I've never been more terrified in my life.

"Oh shut up," Gia said. "And get off the floor. A man crying and on his knees *can* be sexy, and fun," with a wink to me, "but this is just pathetic."

Tony stood up, wiped his eyes and nose, adjusted his collar and cuffs.

"Besides," she went on, "I haven't made macaroons in at least an eon. Maybe two."

Tony tilted his head slightly. "I was going to ask," he said, immediately back to his regular cold self. "Where's all the food? I mean, the cakes and pies and pastries? And the champagne? All I could find were moldy, dusty sugar cookies."

She pouted, and I knew I'd be hard until we got out of here, which needed to happen soon—poor little guy was not enjoying this anymore.

"Fucking management," she said, looking at the floor and spitting, somehow attractively, a strawberry seed. "They were doing a cost-analysis thing, and they figured we didn't need the slug's milk to control these idiots. I mean, they seriously just sit there, gazing into each other's eyes all the time, until they can't take it anymore and just have to touch each other, and then they get burned and the whole thing happens over again. And again, and again. Almost as pathetic as you crying about those macaroons." She looked him in the eye without raising her head. Even I could tell it was a rookie move for someone of her talent and experience. Tony wasn't going to fall for that. "You really miss them that much?" she asked. "My macaroons?"

He paused a beat. They say timing is everything. "Meh. They were decent, I guess. I just needed to make sure you laid off the kid for a minute, let him get back to his senses. Flattery will get you everywhere, right?"

So it had been only an act, Tony's meltdown, and I couldn't have been happier to know it. It would have been nearly impossible to take him seriously after that pathetic scene, and if I was to survive this little tour, I needed him to have his shit together. None of this weeping-on-the-floor nonsense.

She burst out in tears, and this time you're damn right I covered my mouth. "Why are you still so mean to me?" She wailed like she'd seen *Gone with the Wind* a few too many times, the back of her wrist held to her forehead and everything. "It's been so long. Can't you forgive me? You know I feel different about you than any of the others."

I looked at Tony. He looked...bored. "Stop it already, Gia. The GM is expecting us. And you're embarrassing yourself in front of the kid."

She dabbed under her eyes. "Can't blame a girl for trying," she said, cool and calm. It had been an act not unlike Tony's own. "Fine. Leave me here, bored and alone with these sappy, burnt fools. But don't expect me to pine after you anymore. We're done."

"Can I get that in writing?"

She turned her back to him. "Can you just go already?"

"Oh yeah we can." He snapped his fingers and pointed toward the back of the room. "Let's get outta here, kid. And keep your hand right where it is."

He didn't wait for me, just started walking.

I was still looking at Gia, though only from behind—maybe she'd turn around one more time before we left—when she called after him. "Have fun downstairs on your way out, sexy," and then, turning to me with another slow wink, "I'll be waiting right here for you, gorgeous, if you ever make it back. And you'll be leaving the tie on."

That did it—I now needed yet another pair of discount-rack dress pants.

"Let's go, kid!" Tony shouted from a ways away.

I hustled, gooey and warm, after him. Without Gia around, the room was again mostly darkness, but I managed to find him along the back wall, at an elevator. The single glowing button was a down-pointing pitchfork with a devil's tail handle.

"Clever," I said.

"Yeah. They spare no expense. Or, they used to spare no expense."

The elevator door opened, Tony ushered me inside, and down we went. Way down. Long enough the silence became palpable.

"So," I eventually said, steeping in my own shame and ejaculate, "you and Gia, huh?"

He shifted on his feet and cleared his throat, but never took his eyes off the door.

"That must have been...holy shit, I can't even imagine. I mean—"

"Zip it, kid. We won't be—"

"Yeah, yeah. We won't be speaking about this again," I said. "You know, this is gonna get really boring if we can't talk about anything."

He gave me the side-eye. "I can fucking smell you."

I joined him in staring at the door. "Yeah. Sorry. I swear that never happens." I was hoping for at least a chuckle, but got nothing. I glanced over at him. "So, when this opens…"

He remained focused on the door. "When this opens, we stay completely silent and exit to the left. We keep quiet, we keep our backs to the wall, and you follow me close. Hopefully they won't notice we're here."

"Jesus. Hopefully who won't notice?"

Tony was a stone with eyes, staring at that door. "There's a seedier, more awful, more violent side to Lust," he said. "Not everyone here gets to sit comfortably in a room with fireplaces, soft smells, and light jazz. Up there? That's for lustful lovers. Down here is for lustful assholes. Grabassers, goosers. Sometimes—most times—worse. There's nothing romantic about where we're going. Stay close, and we should be fine." He finally chanced a glance away from the door, at me. "Might actually be a good thing, the cum soaking through your slacks. Like camouflage. Still, though, nothing in the mouth."

"Nothing in the mouth," I dutifully repeated as the elevator began to slow.

"This is gonna be nasty, kid," he said, his focus back on the door. "Remember, stay close and stay quiet." He cracked his neck and stole one more deep breath.

Ding. The elevator stopped, and the door slid open to the sound of screams of both pain and violently-taken pleasure, menacing and deep, penetrating. Then the smell of all sorts of bodily fluids. Then the full force of driving drum-and-bass accompanied by strobe lights.

A club. Great.

Tony slid out into the fray, disappearing to the left until his hand reappeared in front of me, again snapping and pointing. I hurried to my spot against the wall beside him, and the elevator closed and went back up, taking its light with it, allowing my eyes to adjust.

The strobe flashed over neon purples and greens and blues. The high-tops and stools were all tall, sharp angles—very chic. A few lounge areas were scattered around the bar, furnished with the obligatory red leather couches and glossy mid-shin-level tables. A DJ spun EDM too loudly from, I don't know, somewhere.

In truth, the space itself wasn't any more offensive than any other club I'd ever been to.

The party raging inside was another story, though. The line at the bar seemed about normal—a bunch of bros clamoring over each other and calling out for Jaegerbombs—until I realized they were all naked and dripping with, well, something that got my hand back to my mouth. And then I slowly realized what was happening out on the floor, and at the high-tops, and in the lounges: a sea of naked men, and only men, lay before me, fucking each other from behind and with all manner of…things. I couldn't begin to count the zucchinis, champagne bottles, and cocks being shoved into all the upturned assholes, the miles of twine tied tightly above purpling testicles, the cheese graters filing away slivers of erect nipple. And that was only at first glance.

Everything and everyone in the room was drenched in a cocktail of bodily fluids, not entirely unlike one of those foam parties these places sometimes throw, even above. And the looks on their faces—sheer joy for the violators, terror and pain for the violated.

I frantically slapped at the wall for the elevator button, but I couldn't find the damn thing.

Tony caught me by my flailing wrist. "Sorry, sport," he said. "This is one of those *the only way out is through* kind of things. We gotta go."

I closed my eyes, took a moment to steel myself, then looked at him and nodded. He nodded back, and off we went, our backs sliding along an unnaturally slick, slimy wall. I kept my eyes closed, trusting I'd simply run into him if he stopped. We were moving slowly enough that a little bump couldn't hurt. I didn't dare open them. The sounds—slapping, thudding, squishing, tearing—the sounds were bad enough.

I lost track of time, like in the void, only much more disgusting. Could have been five minutes, could have been forty. Everything about this place was torture, and torture, I've come to learn, does fucked up things with time.

Then, sudden, terrifying, and way too fucking loud, Tony puked. "Jesus fucking Christ," he spewed, spitting god-knows-what from his mouth, wiping that same god-knows-what from his chin, cheeks, and eyes. "Fucking shit asshole cocksucking mother dick! Right in my fucking mouth!"

I backhanded his shoulder and looked at him accusingly—my eyes must have bulged three inches from their sockets.

His eyes also went wide and, I shit you not, he covered his mouth like a child who's just realized he said a swear in front of his mother.

It went quiet. We both slowly turned to face the room.

Blood-covered, cum-drenched, shit-smelling men, a fucking sea of them, had stopped mid-everything. Their crazy-eyes were now focused on us as their hands clenched tight on whatever sexually deviant implement they held.

The static of a microphone switching on came over the speakers.

"Shit," Tony said.

"Tony!" a voice called over the sound system. "I was wondering when you'd finally come visit."

"Luigi?! Oh, fuck off, man," Tony shouted. "Don't you have a sixteen-year-old hostess to rape in the walk-in?"

It seemed like a bad idea, patronizing this Luigi fellow, but there was nothing I could have done. By this point I was well beyond incapable of speech, let alone movement. I would just have to accept whatever fate was coming for me.

"Look around you," continued the disembodied voice. "I don't waste time with that piddly shit anymore."

"You're a sick, fat, ponytailed, soulless ginger fuck, Luigi. What did you do here?"

Luigi's laughter boomed through the P.A. "I've made a few improvements, is all," he said. "You don't like what I've done with the place?"

"Oh, it's effective. No question this is Hell. And the Jaegerbombs? Nice touch. I'm guessing they think they're doing this to women?"

"Until the slug juice wears off, yeah. God, you should see their faces the moment they sober up and realize it's about to happen to them, too."

"I'm sure the GM's happy with your work," Tony said. "Speaking of which, we're on our way there now, so we'd better get going." Then, under his breath to me, "The door's about thirty yards ahead. Stay close to the wall. Get ready to run, kid. Fast."

I was, of course, already ready to run. Fast.

"You should really meet the boys before you go," Luigi said confidently from wherever he was broadcasting. Smug asshole.

"Shit," Tony muttered, loudly enough for only me to hear. "Sick fuck."

"Boys," Luigi said, "introduce yourselves to Tony and his, uh, friend."

"Go go go go go!" Tony shouted as he took off along the wall.

He had no need to repeat himself like that—I was close enough behind him to be drafting like a fucking

NASCAR driver. Again, I didn't dare look, but I could hear those rapey fucks grunting in pursuit, clicking the salad tongs intended for our nipples or our taints or something, their feet suctioning off the snuff-porn theatre floor.

A slimy digit grazed the back of my neck. "Get a move on, old man," I panted. My rectum, I'd decided, was a space unsuitable for the storage of fresh, or even frozen, produce.

Either he didn't hear me, or he just couldn't be bothered to answer. He charged ahead for what seemed like longer than this supposed thirty yards, never once adjusting his stride or turning his head.

Something pinched the back of my right thigh. Then another pinch, this time on my ass cheek and hard enough I was sure it would leave a mark. I could feel the warmth of their breath, could feel droplets of foulness splashing my face. "Tony Tony Tony Tony Tony Tony go go go go go go go!"

He went. Then suddenly he reached out his left hand, caught the door handle and turned it in one motion as he blew past, and used the door as a sort of emergency break.

I slammed into the thing like a crash test dummy—karma hitting me for that incident back with the Glutton—and Tony shoved me through, diving on top of me as the door swung closed on a hand wielding a fucking immersion blender. I shoved Tony off me, threw all my weight into the door, and wrestled the blending/raping implement from the offending digits before finally getting the door closed and latched.

We were back in the void. I couldn't see it, but I could definitely feel and smell the shit, blood, and cum on my hands.

Tony laughed while trying to catch his breath. "Pierre's gonna be pissed."

"What? Why?"

"We're gonna make a fucking mess of his koi ponds."

SIX

After a slimy silence in the void, the lights came up in the Waiting Room. A woman—no description necessary; you know the kind of which I speak—was screaming, throwing things, and threatening Pierre with a pointed index finger. She was livid about something but seemed, temperature-wise, perfectly comfortable.

"I swear to fucking god I'll have your job," she yelled. "I'm friends with the owner. So give me what I want, or I swear to Christ I'll call her, and by the end of the night you'll be looking for a new job!"

I was covered in filth like I'd never known and couldn't be bothered with this *I know the owner* crap. People who say that are always full of shit. So I took off for the nearest clean koi pond—which took some time, seeing as I'd already soiled so many—shedding clothing with each step, finally down to my boxers and my TIE tie, which was draped over my shoulders and still carrying the scent of Gia. No way I was getting rid of that smell. The sinners continued their waiting unperturbed as I hustled past, finally reaching clean water and immediately submerging my entire head.

The fish, belly-up, bumped my face on their way to the surface almost instantly, and even though I try to be respectful of life in all its forms, I couldn't have cared less. I pulled my head from the water and got to bathing myself, right there in front of everyone.

None of them noticed, of course, focused as they were on their waiting.

Finally clean and mostly naked, I returned to the host stand, where Pierre was still dealing with that woman.

"My apologies, madam," he said. "It seems there was a small issue with scheduling. Your table is ready after all." The red curtains materialized behind him. "Please," he continued, never losing that smile, "enjoy your experience here at The Inferno."

She huffed. "Too late now."

Pierre raised an eyebrow. "Indeed."

She huffed again and strolled confidently through the curtain and the door behind it, which closed without a sound on this side. The door and the curtain vanished.

Tony, somehow already clean and wearing fresh threads, grunted as he forced himself off the wall and out of that Marlboro Man pose he liked so much. "Wrath?" he asked. "Pride?"

"Wrath, of course," Pierre answered. "Wrath like your friend will experience if he continues to soil my decorative ponds and kill my fish."

"Sorry," I said, and I was. "But if you've ever been

where we just—"

"Oh, yes," he said, cutting me off and turning to Tony like I was merely a fly buzzing around the room. "My apologies, Tony. I forgot to tell you that Luigi is now managing the club."

"Yeah," Tony said. "Would have been good to know."

Pierre scoffed. "I cannot be expected to remember everything." He finally noticed I was naked and dripping wet. "*Bordel de merde*," he said, retching. "Clothes for the pale one, first. That is, quite honestly, one of the more disturbing things I've ever had the misfortune to witness." He pressed the clothing rack button, again displaying all the same discount trash for me to choose from.

By this point, quality was of little importance. I just wanted to be covered. So I dressed, leaving the tags attached, you know, just in case.

"Ah yes," Pierre continued, "that is much better. Now, Tony, you knew Besh was on his way out. Things above have changed, and he was unwilling to change with them. Luigi is…progressive, as upper management would call it. He's been waiting centuries to show the GM what he can do, and when he saw his chance to climb down the ladder, he took it. You cannot expect me to believe you did not see this coming."

Tony snatched a toothpick from Pierre's stand and dropped its plastic wrapper to the floor. "We all saw it coming, Pierre," he said. "I just didn't think it would be so soon. I was expecting…and then the elevator door opened and…just seems like a vital piece of information to have passed on, you know? I mean, seeing as you're the fucking maître d'."

"I do not understand all this moaning and whining. You are perfectly fine," Pierre said, looking me over and shaking his head in disgust as I again reaffixed my highly offensive tie. "As is your charge, right down to his dreadful fashion sense. No harm, no foul. That is the saying, no?"

"Yeah. That's the saying." Tony spat the toothpick to the floor as Pierre turned his attention back to his ledger. The toothpick's plastic wrapper, which should have been right there on the floor, was gone, though I hadn't noticed anyone pick it up.

I straightened up and slicked back my still-dripping hair. "How do you know that asshole?" I asked Tony. "And what did you do to piss him off?"

"He's worked here longer than I have, kid. I don't know what to tell you. We just never got along."

Pierre never took his attention from his book, but he harrumphed like it was his native language.

"Got something to add there, Frenchy?"

Pierre looked up at me and then slowly turned to Tony. "Perhaps it is not my place?"

Tony opened his hands in front of him, inviting Pierre's opinion. "Fuck it," he said. "What you got?"

"I am not judging, of course, my friend." I was still pretty sure I couldn't trust Pierre for much, but he sounded sincere to me. "But you did play a rather large role in the postponement of his promotion."

"Oh, come on. You know I had nothing to do with that. All he had to do was back off and leave her alone.

But no. He couldn't stop himself."

Pierre *ahem*-ed, politely, almost. "I am aware," he said. "But you did speak against him to the GM, and you know Luigi. He is precisely the type to hold a grudge."

"Yeah, but enough of a grudge to sick his," Tony paused and shuddered, "his *boys* on me? If the GM found out about that, he'd be right out on his ass."

"So why don't you tell the GM about it when we get there?" I asked, mostly because I was beginning to feel forgotten.

Pierre laughed. *"Tell the GM when we get there,"* he repeated.

"Sorry, kid," Tony said. "Forgot you were there. And no, we won't be telling the GM about any of that. You know that thing they say up above? *Snitches get stitches?*" He waited for me to nod. "Well, we don't bother with a catchy little saying down here. Down here, it's way worse than stitches."

"But didn't you already rat him out once?"

"That was different. I was summoned. And you don't lie to the GM."

I looked at Pierre. "Tony is right," he said flatly. "It is better to leave it in the past."

I was still learning the rules of this place, so I just went along. "So, uh, why did the GM summon you? What's Luigi so pissed about?"

"Jesus, kid. You just don't know when to give it a rest, do you?"

"Something to do with Gia, right?" I asked Pierre.

Pierre looked at Tony. "He will find out eventually, my friend."

"Fine," Tony barked, opening his closet again, distracting himself by leafing through all the fancy duds. "Tell him, but keep it short. We gotta get a move on."

"Of course, Tony." Pierre closed his ledger and called me over with that spooky finger, close enough I didn't think Tony could hear. "I assume you saw the way Tony and Gia responded to one another?" I nodded, so he went on. "Many, many years ago, when Tony was first given his position here, he and Gia…how would you say…*had a thing*. Gia has always been here, has always been powerful. Luigi has also always been here, and he has always found Gia irresistible. So much so that, as his power grew, he became convinced he deserved Gia for himself. He kidnapped her and kept her locked away, and he did things to her you couldn't even comprehend, so I will not bother to explain. She eventually escaped, and although she and Tony kept quiet about it, the GM found out. The GM always finds out. Tony was summoned to give his account of any and all interactions he had witnessed between Gia and Luigi."

Tony slammed the door to his closet. "Get to the point, Pierre. I'm fucking bored already."

Pierre sighed and shook his head. "In the end, Luigi received what essentially equates to a restraining order and a probationary period of, I believe, seven hundred years. He completed his probation, Besh was, shall we say, relieved of his duties, and Luigi now manages the Club."

"Right below Gia," I said. "Damn. I guess working in this business is the same in every realm of existence. Always with the drama. What happened, anyway?"

"Pardon?"

"Tony and Gia? What happened?"

Pierre looked over at Tony and frowned. I could have sworn he actually cared. "That, I do not know. Neither of them will speak of it."

I also looked at Tony. He was just standing there, lost in, seemingly, thought. "Tony? Not speak of it? I never would have guessed."

"We done?" Tony asked, but more like a command. "Hit the button, Pierre."

Pierre hit the button and looked up at me. "If I were you, I would not bring it up again," he said. "And, if you would not mind too terribly, try to stay clean."

SEVEN

"God dammit, kid. I said drop it." Tony suddenly seemed more tired than angry.

"I'm just saying," I said into the darkness, emboldened by Tony's show of vulnerability back in the Waiting Room and realizing I could now get under his skin, "you shouldn't keep your feelings all bottled up. It's not healthy. You can talk to me if you need to."

"Ever been backhanded by an immortal spectral being?"

This was fun. "See? That's what I'm talking about. You drive people away with your anger."

"I don't know if this has ever felt more like Hell."

Before I had time to continue with my smartassed show of support, the click, the whir, the lights. This, however, was no dining room. This was easily the most massive kitchen ever constructed. A row of stainless steel counters lined with brilliant, snow-white cutting boards shimmered out into the distance, bright in the overhead fluorescents, not one of them flickering. The brick-red tiled floor was spotless.

At every station along the unimaginably long lines stood a white-aproned human—or, former human—with surprisingly easy access to all manner of sharp or hot things.

As should be the case in any respectable kitchen, the radio was silent as the cooks slaved away, but it was far from quiet. Behind each of the cooks stood a flame-haired man in a white chef's jacket, veins surging through his forehead and neck. Each chef screamed an endless river of obscenities at the cook before him, his spittle flying to land on the white aprons, dissolving them away with a hiss, a puff of smoke, and a grimace and groan from the cook.

"Before you feel the need to point out the obvious," Tony said, "no, this is not a dining room."

"Holy shit that's a lot of line cooks. And, uh, chefs?"

Tony grinned and breathed a relieved sigh. "Just one chef, actually. But yeah, a lot of him." He raised a hand to shield his eyes from the light and searched the room. "We just have to find—ah, there he is."

"Who?"

"Down there," Tony said, pointing. "The one who isn't screaming his fucking head off."

I followed his finger and saw, maybe fifty yards down the line, the chef Tony was talking about. He was standing with the only person not wearing an apron, who appeared to be waving a white flag.

"So you found him," I said. "And?"

Tony pulled two aprons from their hooks just inside the door. He handed one to me, draped the other over his head, tied the strings around his waist, and strolled onto the line like he owned the place. "We go say hi."

I followed, flanked on either side by the sights, sounds, and smells of a bustling kitchen: wisps of steam rising from pots of boiling water, glints of light reflecting off polished utensils, oil popping in searing hot pans, the scrapes of metal spoons in metal mixing bowls, fresh cut herbs and the potent tang of vinegar.

Over everything, though, the constant rantings and ravings of hundreds of angry chefs—or hundreds of one angry chef—all with the same British accent, same inflection on the same curse words, and same recycled insults. *This lamb is so raw it's about to eat the fucking garnish! This soup is so bland it reminds me of fucking your whore mother! You fucking doughnut!*

I'd been hoping for a more chilled-out experience in this room, but this did not seem to bode well. I called after Tony, but my voice was lost to the din, and he never broke stride. We approached the pair from behind the chef and were upon them in no time.

The chef was, from the back at least, identical to the rest of the chefs, but he wasn't screaming like the others—he was being screamed *at* by the same woman we had witnessed giving Pierre the business back in the waiting room. She had a white apron clenched in one hand while the other sported a wagging index finger, apparently her go-to move for telling people what's what.

"Absolutely not!" she screeched. "I am *so* not here to work! Like I told that foreign piece of shit at the door, I want my regular table, or I'm calling my friend, who *owns* the place. You'll be right out on your ass, you ginger asshole!"

The chef said nothing, but his shoulders jostled. Even from behind, I knew he was laughing.

I looked at Tony, but he was focused on the argument, a grin spread over his face, enjoying this more than I'd seen him enjoy anything yet.

"And another thing," the woman continued, that finger still going, "I don't know who you think you—" She stopped, finally noticing Tony and me over the rising and falling of the chef's shoulders. "What the fuck are you looking at?"

The chef glanced behind him, over his right shoulder. Upon seeing Tony, he spun fully, raised his arms in the unmistakable beginnings of an embrace, and stepped forward, his entire face taken over by a smile. "Tony, you fucking shite! Why didn't you tell me you were—"

The woman caught him by the shoulder. "Oh no you don't," she said, spinning him back around to face her. "I was here first, and we're not finished. Not until you take me—"

The chef spat directly into her mouth, which hissed and smoked as her tongue was eaten away, as her lips dissolved to expose perfectly white and aligned teeth. "Will you kindly shut up now, you mewling fucking quim?"

The woman dropped to her knees and got her hands to what she had left of her face. She was either sobbing or screaming, probably both. Either way, she was far from shutting up.

"Bloody hell," he said, turning again to Tony.

"Sorry, old friend. This will only take a moment."

Tony nodded. "Take your time, Gordo. You know how much I love watching you work."

Gordo nodded and turned back to the crumpled, sizzling woman. He knelt beside her, laid a hand softly on her heaving back, and put his mouth close to her ear. "I must apologize," he said, sliding his hand up her back to her head, gathering her hair in his fingers, and tilting her head up, surprisingly tender about it, so she could see him. "It seems there's been a mistake."

The woman blinked tears from her eyes and nodded her head. Her mouth was now a skeletal grimace, but I got the impression she was trying to smile in agreeance. If her tongue hadn't been burned away, she probably would have said something along the lines of *You're goddamn right there's been a mistake*. Awful fucking human.

"Tony," I said, softly, because I mean, damn, you know? "What the fuck?"

"Zip it, kid," Tony said, his eyes still on Gordo and the woman. "This is when it gets fun."

Gordo tightened his grasp on her hair and used it to lift her until she was at his eye level, her legs kicking six inches off the floor. "You seem to have mistaken me for someone who might give a FLYING FUCKING SQUIRREL'S LEFT FUCKING TESTICLE ABOUT WHAT YOU WANT!" His voice now boomed so loud that everything else was completely drowned out, and it took on a piercing quality that nearly brought me to my knees. "NOW SHUT THE FUCK UP, PUT ON THAT FUCKING APRON, AND WALK YOUR ASS DOWN THIS FUCKING LINE TO YOUR

FUCKING STATION, OR I *WILL* RIP YOUR INTESTINES OUT OF YOUR BLEACHED FUCKING ARSEHOLE AND FEED THEM TO YOU FOR THE REST OF FUCKING ETERNITY!"

After a stunned moment, she peed, sobbed once, and said, "Yaarch."

"YES FUCKING WHAT?!"

"Yaarch, czaach."

"Damn fucking right, *yes, chef.*" He set her down, straightened her hair, and pointed to the apron on the floor beside the puddle of piss. "And clean that up."

Another sob as she again fell to her knees and grabbed the apron. "Yaarch, czaach."

He spun around like nothing had happened and opened his arms in Tony's direction. "How have you been, you fucking cunt? Wish I'd known you were coming. I'd have whipped up something special."

To my astonishment, Tony practically ran into Gordo's embrace, wrapped those impossibly long arms around his back, and gave a succession of forceful slaps. "You'd have had one of the other *you*s whip up something special, you mean. How are things, Gordo?"

Gordo released Tony and took a step back. "No complaints."

Tony threw his chin in the direction of the lines. "See you've done a little restaffing."

"About bloody fucking time, too." Gordo lifted his foot and inspected a droplet of pee that had somehow splashed from the puddle and onto his shoe. He looked at the faceless woman on her knees, sopping up her urine with her apron, shook his head in disgust, and looked back at Tony. "Fucking savages. Anyway, you know how it is when you take over a place. I gave the old staff a fair go of it. Not my fault they were all useless fucking twats."

Tony chuckled. "I'm sure you gave them a real fair go," he said. "Of course, it's not like I've never wanted to run a kitchen full of *me*s."

"I know it seems a wee bit narcissistic," Gordo said, "but holy fucking shite, Tony, no kitchen in history has ever run this smoothly."

"I don't doubt it." Tony looked over at me and shook his head. "Good help is hard to find."

"Oh yes," Gordo said, also turning to me. "My apologies. Who's your petrified friend then?"

"I'm taking him to see the GM."

"Bullshit," Gordo said, sizing me up. "This spooked little cunt? Look at him. He's wearing a bloody Star Wars tie, for fuck's sake."

Tony rubbed his forehead. "Yeah, I know. But we don't have far to go, and he's still here, so, you know."

"Don't have far to go, do you?" Gordo grinned the grin of a villain. "Already seen Gia then?"

"We have."

"And? One last shag in Hell?"

"Fuck off, Gordo," Tony said before snapping his fingers in my face. "Snap out of it, kid. There's nothing to be afraid of here, and you're being rude."

"I'm not afraid," I said, realizing it was the truth. "I'm just…" I offered my hand. "Sorry. Good to meet you, Gordo."

He shook my hand firmly, looking me in the eye. "And you," he said. "I…forgive me, but silence typically means fear here. If you're not bloody fucking terrified, why are you so fucking quiet?"

I looked up and down the line of cooks and chefs. The cooks I'd already figured were the Wrathful, doomed to a punishment I was sure I'd be introduced to soon enough. The chefs, though—clones? Induced hallucinations? I couldn't wrap my head around it.

"I'm just working things out," I said, surprised at my calm. "I get why there's so many, uh, *cooks*. But how are there so many of you? Like, clones or something?"

It was Gordo's turn to rub his forehead. He looked at Tony. "I can't believe the GM, with all that infinite fucking wisdom, wants to see a sci-fi nerd."

Tony shrugged.

Gordo sighed. "Each one is another me, though I doubt you'll understand that, seeing as you share sixty percent of your DNA with a fucking banana."

It was my turn to chuckle.

"What the fuck are you laughing at?" Gordo demanded, his face going radish red.

"I like the way you say ba*nah*na. Now say sha*llots*."

He opened his mouth to speak, but he laughed instead. "Nevermind, Tony," he said, catching his breath. "I get why the GM wants to see him. He's an arsehole, just like you."

Tony flipped him off. "Wrath begets wrath, kid," he said. "Gordo and I went to school together. I thought about going for this job, actually. But he's always had this gift. Anger and vengeance and a general sense of violent *arse*holery just kind of spill out of him. So much that it eventually becomes another of him. Looks like you've really learned to harness that, eh Gordo?"

"Again, about bloody time." Gordo spat, for apparently no reason, onto the back of the woman still sopping up urine. Bladder of a horse, that one. The spit ate through her clothes and got to her skin, which popped and sizzled like the sounds still coming off the line. She arched her back but didn't make a peep. That voice of his was fucking powerful. "But," he continued, "it was mostly out of necessity. You been above lately, Tony? These people, fuck are they angry. That's why I had to replace the staff. Lesser demons can't handle this kind of volume."

"Heard that," Tony said. He took another glance around the kitchen. "I gotta say, you've done one hell of a job here, bud."

I groaned. "Okay. I've had about enough of this long-lost romantic reunion shit. I'm gonna go check out the kitchen and let you two catch up or whatever. That cool?"

But they had already forgotten me, already dived headfirst into the deep, deep pool of nostalgia that eternity must inevitably fill. So I just walked off, heading for the first station I came across, which happened to be sauté. The cook had his back to me, facing the stovetop and stirring something in a pan.

The cook's own personal Gordo stood about a foot behind him, hissing insults and spitting acid, searing the clothes off the cook's back and the skin off his bones. "Are you seriously stirring that with the handle of the fucking spoon?"

"Yes, Chef!" answered the cook as best he could

through clenched teeth.

"You're a fucking embarrassment!" continued Gordo the Lesser, the spittle flying. "Your Neanderthal parents should be fucking ashamed of themselves!"

"Yes, Chef! I'm sure they are, Chef!"

I cleared my throat, and Little Gordo turned around. "Hold on a tick," he said to me before turning back to the cook. "Fucking disgraceful! Lick that pan clean and start again."

"Yes, Chef!" answered the cook as he turned down the heat.

"Did I say to take it off the burner?"

"No, Chef!" The cook turned the heat back up, bent over at the waist, and commenced licking. It smelled something like a burning hotdog.

Gordo turned back to me. "Useless," he said. "The lot of 'em."

"Yeah, I wanted to ask…so, back there—"

"How can it be I'm talking to you and your friend Tony simultaneously? It's bloody simple, really. You see—"

I cut him off with a head shake. "No. That part I get just fine. Different reality or whatever."

"What the fuck are you talking about?"

"Tony. He told me…" I paused, noting the slightly confused look on Gordo's face. "He just explained the way things work here, more or less. What I was going to ask—"

He raised a hand to cut me off. "Who are these cooks, and why are they here? Well you see—"

"No," I interrupted. "I get that, too. They're sinners.

The Wrathful, if I had to guess. Like that woman whose mouth he, or you, burned off and made clean her own piss, always screaming at the help like a fucking asshole." I looked over to the pan-licker, who, to his credit, was being thorough about his work. "And you weren't wrong when you said that thing about how angry people are. It's a fucking shitshow up there, man. A world of angry, entitled fucking douchebags."

Gordo whistled. "I gotta say, kid, I'm impressed. I thought you'd be much more uncomfortable once you got up close, but you're cold as the middle of an Applebee's steak."

"Ha. Nice," I said. "And if it's cold, it's cold, but I think these fuckers got what they deserve. You wouldn't believe how many times I've wanted to spit in the mouth of a screaming customer."

"I can see why Tony likes you." He smiled and pulled a meat thermometer from the little pocket on his sleeve, unsheathed it from its plastic sheath. "Care to give him a little jab?"

I took the thermometer from him and again looked at the cook. "I don't know," I said. "I mean, I'm kinda just along for the ride here, you know?"

"Don't be a fucking chickenshit," Gordo said. "I know that look in your eyes. And you've nothing to fear. You're perfectly safe."

"Well, if you insist." I took a step forward, but hesitated. "Anywhere?"

"Anywhere. And make it bloody hurt. It's bloody fucking Hell, after all then, innit?"

I stepped up to the stove to find that the cook had

finished licking the searing hot pan clean. He looked surprised to see me and uttered a stream of unintelligible mumbles, his lips sausage skins forgotten over open flame, his tongue swollen and oozing that bloody puss that comes with a bad burn.

I mocked him with a hand to my ear. "I'm sorry, you piece of fucking shit, what was that?"

He repeated himself, I think, but louder this time, screaming at me the way he must have screamed at customer service folk of every ilk while he was still alive.

In his face I saw the faces of hundreds of irrationally irate customers from my past, cursing, slamming fists into bars and tabletops, insulting my intelligence and my profession. Years of these loathing and loathsome pricks. Fucking decades, man.

I stabbed that motherfucker straight through the eye, the thermometer's face wedged into the socket where his eye had just been. He howled and fell into the stove, knocking the pan to the floor, the flames cooking the side of his face with the new eye until he finally collapsed to the floor.

I knew it wouldn't have quite the same effect as when Gordo did it, but I spit on him anyway. It just felt right.

"Bloody fucking brilliant!" Gordo slung his arm over my shoulders. "I mean, way to commit, young man. You hesitated back there, and I thought you were gonna back out or poke him in the arm or something, but—just fucking brilliant." He dropped his arm, stooped over the fallen cook, and looked back at me. "Felt fucking good, too, d'innit?"

I sighed and smiled.

"Thought it might have," Gordo said. He slapped the cook's crispy cheek, once, hard. "What the fuck are you doing on the fucking floor?! Get the fuck up and get back to work, you lazy fucking arsehole!"

"Yaarch, czaach!"

"Damn right, *yes chef*." Little Gordo caught the cook by the chin and looked him over. "I think I prefer him this way. Shame to lose the thermometer, but I haven't done any actual cooking in years anyway."

He released the cook, who immediately got back to work, hiding his face from me in the process.

"Just fucking brilliant," Gordo said again. "You had a question, yeah?"

I'd never stabbed anyone before, let alone through their eye and half their fucking brain, but I'd always imagined that sort of thing would, if not kill a person, at least incapacitate them. Logically, I understood that he was already dead, and therefore he couldn't die again. Or maybe they wouldn't let him die again because then there would be nothing left to torture.

It was a lot to process, so it took me a moment. "I, uh…yeah. I think I got my answer."

Little Gordo nodded. "Ah. No, the dead can't die. And Tony's asking me to send you back to us. He says it's time to go."

"Okay," I said, glaring over his shoulder at the cook.

"Wanna spit on him again? You know, one last *fuck you* for the road?"

"Yes," I said, hocking one up and speaking with a mouthful of warm loogy. "Yes I do."

EIGHT

We'd exited the kitchen through the mop room, which housed the usual array of cleaning solution dispensers, floor sink, and great host of soiled mop heads, and were again in the void.

"Through the eye with a meat thermometer, eh?" Tony said. "I didn't think you had it in you."

"You saw that?"

"Gordo was giving me the play-by-play. Amazing how he can do that...." He trailed off in thought for a moment. "I do wish I'd have seen it, though. Imagining that asshole with a thermometer for an eye—fucking brilliant. Did the gauge move at all?"

"I honestly wasn't paying attention." And I hadn't been. Jamming a three-inch needle through a man's eye was enough detail for me. I didn't know I had it in me, either, and was still figuring out how guilty I felt about it, if at all. The guy didn't die, so no harm/no foul and all, but still, that was not my typical behavior. "I need a fucking cigarette."

"Kick your right foot out to the side."

I did, and it barely clipped something solid, which bounced with a plastic thump. Having been sold on the idea that nothing existed in the void, I jumped, startled and glad Tony couldn't see. "The fuck?"

"Milk crate," Tony said. "All chefs need a place to escape for a smoke. Gordo more than most."

I bent down and groped with outstretched fingers until they found the latticework of the crate, which I like to imagine was orange. The black ones just don't feel the same, you know? And a pox upon the brown ones... Anyway, it was instinct to pick the thing up and feel around underneath, where I finally found a pack of smokes. I flipped the lid to find one cigarette and a lighter inside.

"Shit. Only one left."

"Come on, kid," Tony huffed, "you should know better than that by now. Think."

I thought. "That last smoke replenishes itself every time he smokes it. And I bet this shitty lighter never runs out of fluid, right?"

"Now you're getting it. Figures it would be Gordo who brought it out of you."

"Dude," I said, lighting the smoke by feel—because apparently even fire can't penetrate that kind of dark—and returning the lighter to its place in the empty pack, which was no longer empty, the replacement cigarette already having materialized. "What's with the hard-on for that guy?"

"Look, kid, friends are few and far between in this place. When you find one, it's best to maintain that relationship. Give it a few thousand years, you'll know what I mean."

I thought about the friendships I'd maintained above, which didn't take long. The restaurant life is a transient life, which makes long-term friendships difficult. Once you've been at one place for a while, it does feel like a little family—dysfunctional and sometimes a bit incestuous, but a family nonetheless. You can't stay there forever, though, and no matter how close you've become with that particular restaurant family, after a year or so you tend to only hear from each other sporadically on social media sites. There are exceptions, of course, but not for me. I couldn't think of a single person I'd have been excited to see at that moment.

I dragged deep from the cigarette. "Fair enough."

The lights came up as I exhaled. All the same people waiting, same elevator music hanging in the air, Pierre at his podium scribbling furiously in his ledger.

"How many more stops do we have left?" I asked.

Tony took the cigarette from my lips and hit it while counting with his fingers. "Three," he said, returning the cig, "if we're counting the GM's office."

"Nice. I can handle that."

Halfway there, not too shabby. I suppose it could have been the nicotine fix, but more likely it was stabbing that guy in the face, the purging of decades of anger and hatred, the reckoning my poor little server/bartender's heart had long been longing for. Either way, for the first time since arriving at The Inferno, I felt at least cautiously optimistic.

Pierre slammed his ledger closed loudly enough to get our attention over the din of the waiting sinners. "Just what do you think you're doing?"

Tony strolled up to the podium, picked up a mint, and popped it in his mouth. "Kid's had a hell of a day, Pierre," he said. "I thought he could use a smoke."

"Not in my waiting room, he can't." Pierre snatched the bowl of mints and hid it inside the podium. He looked at me. "I'm afraid I'll have to ask you to put that out. This is a nonsmoking establishment."

I watched the smoke rise from the the cigarette and then looked over at Tony, who shrugged and shook his head. "You can't be serious," I said.

"Has anything about our previous interactions given you the impression that I am ever anything other than serious?"

I considered, again watching the smoke. "Other than the mustache, I guess not." I scanned the room for an ashtray, but, this being a nonsmoking establishment, I found none. The nearest koi pond was only a few feet away, though, so I took another hit and walked over, flicked the half-wasted smoke into the water.

"No no no no no!" shouted Pierre. "Not in the—" The butt hit the water with a hiss, and Pierre narrowed his eyes at me. "They've only just finished cleaning that. Along with the others you've managed to soil."

I stepped up to the again sparkling-clean pond, the colorful koi swooping above and below one another, and plucked the soggy white stick from the water before it could be swallowed by one of the fish. "Sorry," I said. "But look, we got through that last room perfectly clean. No soiling your koi ponds this time. Other than the cigarette, I mean."

"You will understand if I am less than thrilled."

"Jesus, Pierre," Tony said, sucking on his mint, "what crawled up your ass?"

Pierre gathered himself, but only just. "I am sorry, Tony. It appears there was a fire at one of the larger, gaudier, chain restaurants in Miami. Over three hundred dead, and, of course, many of them will be ending up here. Short notice to prepare for so many."

I made my way up to the podium. "Can't they just wait here? This is a waiting room, right?"

Pierre reached under the podium, pulled out a small wastebasket, and held it out to receive the soggy butt. "Technically, yes," he said, returning the basket to its proper place, "but I would very much like to avoid that. That many sinners milling around would be quite disruptive."

"Disruptive? To who, these assholes? Who cares if their waiting gets disrupted?"

Pierre reopened his ledger and got back to work. "Nobody cares about them," he said. "It would be disruptive to me. They're coming from Miami. I'm in no mood to deal with a horde of humans even more horrible than those already in this room." He glanced up at me. "Present company excluded, of course."

"Wait," I said. "Are you saying I'm more horrible than these people? Or are you saying you don't mind dealing with me?"

He went back to scribbling. "Whichever you prefer, of course."

Tony laughed. "All right, kid. Let's get a move on and let Pierre get this sorted out."

Without a word, Pierre pressed his magic button and the curtain appeared.

"Good luck, man," Tony said, gently slapping the surface of the podium. "And Gordo said to say hi, by the way."

Without looking up, Pierre said, "It was Wrath, then? How lovely for you. And how is your—what do the Americans call it?"

"Bromance," I said, taking a toothpick for the road. "We call it a fucking bromance."

Pierre chortled. "Of course. Bromance. Still going strong, Tony?"

"It's not a fucking bromance, and fuck you both." Tony shot a look at me. "Get moving, kid."

Pierre laughed again and got back to work as Tony and I headed for the door.

"I mean, Gordo's not exactly the looker Gia is," I said, "but you really could do a lot worse."

"Worse than the literal embodiment of wrath? Really?"

"I'm just saying, other than the anger and violence and everything, he seems like a pretty decent guy."

NINE

Click, whir, lights, and we were in an elementary school cafeteria. A sneering red devil logo loomed large on the back wall, the room was lined with glass cases containing various art class creations—rudimentary sculptures of Cerberus and the like—and a stainless-steel buffet line sat empty with no one in line. Everyone had already found their seats, and even without the lunch ladies and their ladles, they each had a tray of food.

The lack of music threw me a little. All the other guests, at least in the dining rooms, had so far been treated to some sort of unending soundtrack, much like the never-changing playlist in any number of places I'd worked over the years. That shit can drive you crazy—only one of the ways this reality mirrored the other.

I picked a red plastic tray from the stack at the end of the buffet line and examined it, drummed my fingers on its edge. "Well this doesn't look so terrible."

Tony took the tray and put it back on the stack. "Yeah. This should be quick and painless. Let's just breeze through this one, yeah?"

If I'd ever again wanted to find myself in a school cafeteria, I'd have quit this business long ago, married, and knocked up my wife. "Fine by me," I said, already looking for the exit. "The way out is through, right?"

Tony half-smiled. "It's the only way, kid."

We walked straight ahead, past a counter laden with plastic cups, each imprinted with the devil mascot and packed full of crayons. Beside the cups, stacks of segmented plastic trays meant to hold cardboard pints of milk and scoops of whatever the school was serving for lunch that day.

The people seated at the tables did not face said tables. Rather, they straddled the bench-seating and were writing on the naked back of the person in front of them, who in-turn wrote on the back of the next in line, and so on. They muttered to themselves as they feverishly scrawled on their neighbor's skin, every so often pausing to pop a chicken nugget into their mouths, but then getting right back to work.

"Remember that deal we made when we first got here?" I asked, definitely too sheepishly. "About me not asking so many questions?"

"I do."

"You're just gonna make me figure this one out, aren't you?"

"I am."

"Is it because I made fun of your bromance with Gordo?"

"It's not a fucking bromance," he said. "And I'm not that petty. Honestly, I want to see what you got.

We've been here long enough you must be starting to figure things out at least a little."

"Alright, old man." I was still riding that wave of optimism from the thermometer incident. "But I'm gonna need a closer look."

"Knock yourself out," he said, offering me the room with his hand. "But remember—"

"Nothing in the mouth, and somebody somewhere is sick of her shit."

"Yeah," Tony chuckled. "Nothing in the mouth. That second part, though, I don't think it's quite as important when it comes to Hot Rod."

"Hot Rod?"

"I'm sure you'll see." He gave me a little nudge. "Go ahead. Look around. I'm just gonna go check out the trophy case, see if they still have anything from when I came through here." And off he went, leaving me to wonder exactly what trophies they gave elementary school students in Hell.

I turned my attention to the cafeteria. I'd waited on plenty of writers in my time, their laptops open on the bar or table, notebooks dangerously close to being ruined by a spilled coffee or beer, their lips moving along with their fingers as they either hit the keys or got pens to paper. I'd long ago learned that it is impolite to interrupt a person mid-wording, but these people here were no longer people. They were sinners. If I was going to impress Tony by figuring out what was going on here, I'd have to unlearn what I had learned.

I picked out a particularly sweaty and focused man about halfway down the table and bent down so my chin was just above his left shoulder, where I'd be able to read what he was putting down.

He seemed not to notice, went on muttering to himself. "Overcooked…harsh lighting…too long of a wait…overpriced for what you get…"

I skimmed over the back in front of him to find that, although he was indeed writing with crayon, this was not your typical crayon. It seared the words into the skin, the smell reminiscent of Gordo's spit hitting bare flesh: *Overcooked…harsh lighting…too long of a wait…overpriced for what you get…*

Not a writer, then. A fucking reviewer.

"Excuse me," I said, no longer caring about interrupting, "can I ask what you're writing?"

He threw down his crayon, popped a waffle fry, and washed it down with some milk, not losing a single drop from the cardboard spout. "Do you have any idea how rude that is? I'm not just sitting here wasting my time, you know."

I eyed the cup of crayons—judging by the way they could slice through backfat, any one of which would have been good for inflicting pain. "Sorry," I said. "I just…You seem like you have more passion about whatever it is you're writing than these people do." Nothing like a good stroke of the ego to get a writer, especially a writer of restaurant reviews, to open up. "I couldn't help myself. I need to know what you're working on."

He took another swig of his milk. "What, these hacks? I don't even know how I'm in the same room as these talentless, tasteless buffoons. Most of them aren't even three-star trusted reviewers. Just hicks who come in from the sticks once a month to eat a meal they don't have to prepare for themselves. Not like me." He went back to writing.

I snuck a glance at the back two sinners down, like cheating on a test, and the text read much like his own. "Not like you?"

As he neared the bottom of his freckled page, its owner ate his last nugget and waffle fry, and the words up by the shoulder blades healed themselves, a CTRL+A+DELETE kind of deal. "I travel for a living," my supposedly professional reviewer said, moving his crayon to the top of the re-fleshed page. "I eat out every day of my life. Expense account, you know? I know restaurants better than anyone. If I can help someone find a half-decent place to eat, all this effort is worth it. I mean, let's be honest here. How hard can it be to provide a good meal and good service at a reasonable price?" He became more agitated as he spoke, unintentionally breaking his crayon, then picking out a new one—burnt sienna, though it didn't seem to make much of a difference. "The people can trust me. How else will they know where to go and actually have a good experience?"

"How altruistic of you," I said, suddenly wishing I carried at least one meat thermometer with me at all times. "Ever worked in a restaurant?"

"Sorry?"

"Bussed tables? Hosted? Prep cook? Dishwasher?"

"Oh god no," he said, waving his hand, shooing away the very thought.

"Any kind of service job? Like a summer at the Gap

or something. Like back in college? You know, even if it was just to get the employee discount?"

Even with the conversation, his latest draft was already a few vertebrae long. "Never. Why would you even ask that? Do I seem like the kind of person who would lower themselves to that kind of work?"

I stood up and stared at the back of his head, now noticing his bald spot, a fine target. "No," I said, clenching a fist and fully prepared to start pounding away. "No you don't."

I was cocked and ready to unleash more of whatever Gordo had inspired in me, but then I heard a voice a little ways down the table. "Welcome to Tastyville!"

I spun to find what basically amounted to a centaur, only with the bottom half of a worm instead of a horse. He wore an apron with an obnoxious flame pattern. His eyes were shielded by equally obnoxious sunglasses—the curved, athletic kind with the reflective, red-tinted lenses. His hair was bleached blond except for the brown roots, its spikes held in place by entirely too much product. He pushed a cart along in front of him, steam rising from the gaps between hotel pans, and stopped at every sinner to scoop more nuggets, fries, and beans onto the trays. With every scoop he energetically repeated, "Welcome to Tastyville!"

"What the fuck is that?" I asked my traveling restaurant critic friend.

"Possibly the worst server I've ever had," he said without looking up from his work. "No personality, and certainly no service standards. I mean, he hasn't asked me once how my food is—it's terrible, by the way. He doesn't tell us the specials, doesn't give us fresh linens. Nothing. He just shows up, welcomes us to Tastyville, and plops this mushy, overcooked crap onto our trays. He never brings fresh trays, either. I swear, I don't even know why I still come here."

"I wouldn't be too hard on him," I said, for some reason pitying the half-worm guy. "This is a really big section."

"Whatever," he said. "He sure as shit isn't getting a tip, and you better believe he'll be showing up in my review of this place, if I can ever manage to get this first page finished."

"Welcome to Tastyville!" the thing said, loading up my new friend's tray with a smile before noticing I was there. He looked at me, and although I couldn't see his eyes through those sunglasses, I had the distinct impression he was confused. After an awkward few moments, he scooped some nuggets from the cart, offered them to me, and asked, "Welcome to Tastyville?"

"Oh," I said, rubbing my belly. "No thanks. I'm full."

"Welcome to Tastyville?" he repeated, frowning, again lifting his serving spoon, like insisting.

I politely raised a hand and shook my head no. "Seriously, I couldn't eat another bite. Thank you, though."

He lowered his head and dumped the heaping spoonful of nuggets back into the cart. "Welcome to Tastyville," he said, sounding defeated.

I thought maybe he was about to cry, which, knowing this place, probably would have been bad. "For real," I said. "I'm just too full. Everything's been wonderful though, really. You've taken excellent care of me. Thank you."

He beamed. "Welcome to Tastyville!"

"Uh, yeah," I said, forcing a smile of my own. "Who doesn't love Tastyville, right?"

"Jesus fucking Christ!" shouted my new friend, so agitated that he dropped his crayon to the floor. "How am I supposed to get this done when you won't shut up back there? People are depending on me."

The crayon bounced near my foot. I looked down and saw that it had come to rest against a thumb, which was connected to a hand, an arm, a body. The benches weren't benches—they were people, on all fours, faces pressed into the asses of the people in front of them. And no matter how any of the sinners sitting on their backs shifted or adjusted, the human bench never flinched, never made a peep.

I bent down to pick up the crayon and get a closer look. The bench-people were fully clothed, so at least this wasn't a Human Centipede kind of deal, and although I couldn't see much of their faces, the look in their eyes wasn't what I'd expected—they weren't frightened or in pain. They were just bored.

I got back to my feet and handed the crayon to the critic. "What about the seating?" I asked. "I mean, I already know what you think about the food and the service, but are you at least comfortable?"

He shifted his ass on the back of the man beneath him and considered. "Now that you mention it, no. What kind of place makes you straddle a bench? And on top of that, I don't even think the thing is cushioned. Great. That's a whole 'nother page I'm gonna have to write."

"Welcome to Tastyville!" Hot Rod exclaimed while replenishing my friend's notepad's tray.

The man ate a waffle fry, and his back healed up again, erasing the few paragraphs the critic had written. He didn't seem particularly upset about it, simply took a breath, ate a fry of his own, and moved his crayon back up to shoulder-level. "Are we done here? I'd like to finish this."

"Listen, asshole," I started. But then I noticed Tony across the table, only visible from the eyes up, peeking out at me between the heads of two sinners.

"Tony? Why are you—?"

Bastard fucking shushed me. "You think I'd be hiding like this if I wanted him to see me? Jesus, kid."

"Okay," I whispered back, nodding towards a door I assumed was the exit.

Tony shook his head no, snatched a nugget off a tray, and threw it at Hot Rod's head.

Pulling the nugget off the spike of hair that had impaled it, Hot Rod spun to find who had thrown the thing, and Tony sprung up from behind his wall of sinners.

"Welcome to Tastyville, my man!" shouted my guide, nearly as excited as he had been to see Gordo.

Hot Rod grinned like he couldn't contain himself. "Welcome to Tastyville! Welcome to Tastyville. Welcome to Tastyville?" He offered Tony a scoop of chicken nuggets.

"Good to see you, too, big guy! And you're right.

It's been too long. I'm good on the nuggets, though."

The smile disappeared from Hot Rod's face as he lowered the spoon. "Welcome to Tastyville?"

"I'd love to, buddy, really. But I have to get this kid to the GM's office right away. We're in kind of a rush. I'm really glad I got to see you, though, big guy." Tony took a step forward, and although I'm sure he'd never admit it, I think it was to give Hot Rod a hug.

Hot Rod was having none of it, though. He slammed his spoon against the table, limp nuggets sent flying, and screamed, "WELCOME TO TASTYVILLE! TASTYVILLE!"

Tony stopped dead, raised his hands in a calming fashion. "Easy, bud. Easy. No need for that kind of language. I promise I'll come back right after, huh? We can sit down and have some of those ice cream cups with the paper lids and tiny wooden spoons. Our hands will look huge, man. I hope you have some of the strawberry ones around here somewhere."

Right back to that big grin. "Welcome to Tastyville! Welcome to Tastyville." That second one with a glance my way.

"I won't bring him. It'll just be you and me. I promise." He grabbed a nugget off the table and tossed it into his mouth. "Mmm...welcome to Tastyville!"

Hot Rod applauded and laughed. "Welcome to Tastyville!" he said once more before going back to moving down the line, feeding the sinners.

I looked at Tony. "That was amazing, man! You're like the Han Solo to his Chewbacca."

"How old are you?" he asked, nodding towards the

door, then heading that way. "Shouldn't you be beyond the Star Wars references by now?"

"I use it as a filter to help me cope with a rather trying reality," I said, hoofing it to keep up. "Fucking deal with it. Why are we walking so fast?"

"Because I need to get you to the GM's office at least close to on-time, kid. Not only because I'm a professional, but also because he's the fucking GM of Hell. Not someone you wanna piss off, you know?"

Seemed reasonable. "Oh. I thought maybe you were just in a hurry to get away from Mr. Conversation back there. I mean, seriously, what was that? *Welcome to Tastyville*? And the hair and that whole getup? Christ."

Tony got to the door but didn't open it. He spun around, towered over me, and did not look pleased. "Look, kid. I understand that all you were able to take away from his part of that conversation was *welcome to Tastyville*, but you've got that stupid human brain, remember? It's not Rod's fault that you're neurologically unable to comprehend a higher form of communication. And as for the getup—yeah, it's not great. But you're wearing a tie with a fictional fucking spaceship on it, so how about you back off?"

I had no idea he could take anything this personally. "Whoa. Yeah, you're right. I'm sorry, ok?"

But he wasn't finished with me. "I mean, fucking people, man. So he dresses a little weird and does that stupid thing with his hair. So fucking what? Yeah, he's odd, and he's maybe not what you'd expect from a fairly high-ranking demon, but nobody slings the way Hot Rod slings. In this business, you are how you do the job. You know that. And you of all people should know that this business is a home for misfits, for the misunderstood. Show a little respect, yeah?"

He totally had me with that. "You're right. Of course you're right. Really, Tony, I apologize."

"Okay then," he said, kicking the door open with the heel of his boot. "Let's get a move on."

TEN

"He's the Glutton's little half-brother," Tony told me as we waited for the waiting room lights to come up. "They're the GM's cousin's kids—or something like that. Some of the other demons will tell you he got the gig out of straight nepotism, but I'm telling you, that pointy-haired S.O.B. can handle his shit. Being the GM's kin might have got his foot through the door, but the rest was all him. That's a tight ship he's running in there."

"If you say so," I said. "I mean, I guess you'd know better than I would."

"It's always going to be that way, kid." Smug bastard. "So, where were we?"

I didn't have to think about it for even a second. "Pride. If we're following the traditional deadly sins model, that was definitely Pride."

Tony put a hand on my shoulder, gave it a little jostle. "Not bad. What gave it away?"

"Are you kidding?" I asked, all full of bravado. "Yelpers? Nobody I've ever met is more full of themselves than somebody who goes online and anonymously rips apart every aspect of a business they know nothing about. Even the good reviews—fuck those people. Do doctors' offices get one-star reviews after making people wait an hour after their scheduled fucking appointments? No. But if a table isn't ready the moment they show up for their dinner reservation, everyone with a fucking internet connection just has to hear about it. This is people's livelihoods these assholes are fucking with, and all because they think they're so much better, so much more important, than *the help*. Like they've never made a mistake at work. Only when they file the wrong report or whatever, I'm not there with my fucking cellphone, immediately posting about their shitty job performance. Yeah. That was definitely Pride."

Tony smiled. "Good to get that one off your chest?"

I didn't say anything. I'd used up all my air for that little tirade. He wasn't wrong about how good it felt to let it out, though. Fuck those people.

Tony was content to let me catch my breath. "Eventually they'll have their own dining room," he said. "The internet's forced renovations in a lot of Hells, and that shit takes time. The cafeteria was the only room big enough to use in the interim, so we just stuck 'em in there for now. Now that I think about it, we never even had a room for Pride until the internet came about. But now that everyone has the opportunity to make their voices heard—let's just say most of them probably shouldn't."

"No argument there," I said. "I have two questions,

though, if that's okay."

"Shoot."

"The crayons—Gordo spit?"

"My man. They mop up whatever doesn't make it to the sinners, wring it out, and mix it with something—I've never asked what—to harden it up."

"Who mops it up? I haven't seen a cleaning crew or anything."

Tony pondered for a moment. "We'll get to the, uh, *cleaning crew* a little later. I wouldn't be surprised if you knew one or two of them, actually."

I was going to press him about this unseen cleaning crew, especially if I might have known some of them, but the lights came up, and the madness before us struck me speechless.

The waiting room was packed to the koi's gills, a horde of leathery-skinned, recently deceased Floridians waiting impatiently for Pierre to take them to their respective tables. They tussled with each other and with the perpetual waiting. They shouted curses at poor Pierre, who took it as well as any Frenchman closing his eyes and thinking of England possibly could have.

Tony let out a long whistle. "I'm sure Pierre's lovin' this."

"Oh, I bet." I took a quick glance at the size of the line. "Should we just jump to the front, or…?"

Tony crossed his arms and leaned back in thought, a smirk developing on his thin lips. "Not the front. Let's just cut in here and let him get through a little more of the line. What was question two?"

I'd forgotten I had a second question. "Right. The

bench people."

"I was wondering when we'd get around to them."

"You know, at first I thought that would also be a good punishment for the prideful—some ironic thing having to do with talking out of their own asses or whatever—but they didn't seem to mind it so much. And if they don't mind it, then it's not really torture, you know?"

"Alright. You know those people who sit at their table an hour after close?" he asked. "Nursing their last two sips of water while the staff is sweeping the floor and flipping the chairs? Or any campers, really. Not to mention those schmucks that are *never* ready to order, or are perpetually late for reservations? They're the Slothful. We tried a handful of harsher, more labor-intensive punishments for them, but they're so oblivious to everything that nothing seemed to work. It was frustrating for the whole staff, really. Got to be so bad for morale that now we just use them as furniture wherever they're needed. There were a few back in Lust, but I guess you were a little, you know, distracted."

At first, the severity of their punishment seemed far too lenient. But then I thought about it. These were the kinds of assholes who would show up five minutes before the kitchen closed and order a well-done steak. Or they'd be the last people in the dining room—the staff standing cross-armed, waiting to clean the table so they can go the fuck home, the manager bringing up the lights and switching off the music. *Oh my god*, they'd say, *are you closing up?* And it wasn't like they'd be snarky about it—they honestly just didn't care about, or notice, the world around them.

Tony was right—no matter the punishment, it would have been wasted on them.

Satisfied, I turned my attention to those in line. "So you've been riding me pretty hard with all the little quizzes and shit," I said. "And I think I've been a pretty good sport about everything, all things considered."

He eyed me suspiciously. "Yeah? And?"

"And I think maybe it's your turn, is all." I opened my hand and presented the room. "Where are these people going?"

He briefly surveyed those in line before looking back at me. "I'm not here to play games, kid."

"Don't give me that shit," I said, crossing my arms. "If you don't know, you don't know. There's no shame in that. You can just admit it."

"It's unwise to test the gods, you know."

I laughed, trying to egg him on. "Come on. We both know you're not a god. Now, an ancient and cranky incorporeal being, sure. But not a god."

"Nice try, kid, but it's impossible to peer pressure anyone who's got thousands of years more experience than you do." He snuck another look at the people in line. "But, as long as we're just waiting in line and all. Forty-eight gluttons. Thirty-four for Lust—twenty-two upstairs, twelve for Luigi to sink his teeth into. Twenty-nine for Pride. Twenty-one for Wrath—aww, good for Gordo. Nine are gonna be stuck in the ranch. And one addition to the cleaning crew."

"Stuck in the ranch? Where's that?"

"You'll see soon enough." I expected a wry grin

with that, but he looked serious.

"Fair," I said. "But I think maybe you missed a few there, Almighty Tony. You can't tell me none of these pricks are slothful."

"I didn't miss anybody. The slothful just aren't in line yet," he said with a wink.

"You're full of shit."

"Have I lied about anything yet?"

"I guess not. But that was—"

"We're almost through the line," he said. "Don't trust me? Ask Pierre."

To my surprise, we were indeed nearly to the podium. And I want to make this clear: no matter what impression I've given of Pierre thus far, I'm telling you right now that his professionalism was unmatched. Sinner after sinner he dealt with, managing complaints and getting on the phone to straighten out any issues, seating this walk-in hundred-ish-top with an almost alarming efficiency. Every restaurant on Earth would run more smoothly if they had their own Pierre.

"Dude's definitely a beast," I said of the maître d'. "And you know I'm gonna ask him."

"Ask him what?" asked the person behind us, a youngish man who must have been close to the heart of the fire, judging by the way the melted skin hung loose off his face. "Why we've been in this line so fucking long? I mean, Jesus. How hard is it to show people to their tables? This place is obviously a shit-hole. If they had wi-fi in here, I'd be leaving a review as we speak. Guess I'll have to wait 'til I get home tonight."

I exchanged a look with Tony, all eyebrows raised,

before responding to the man. "Yeah, good luck with that," I said with a little chuckle.

The man shoved me in the chest, knocking me a few feet out of the line, my back now against the wall beside the nearest koi pond. "The fuck you laughing at, you nerdy little shit? You think I won't beat your ass just coz we're in line at some fancy-pants, overpriced restaurant that can't seat for shit? I swear to fucking God, if you even—"

Tony grabbed him from behind and thrust his entire head into the koi pond, holding him under as he spoke to me. "Okay," he said, "so maybe I'm a little rusty. Looks like this one might bounce back and forth between Pride and Wrath."

I straightened my tie, amazed the thing was still intact. No way an Imperial fighter pilot would have ever made it this far. "Huh," I said. "Some god."

"You know, kid, even the gods aren't infallible. How else do you explain the existence of humanity? Or the Gobblerito?" He was still holding the man under the water. "Thanksgiving dinner wrapped in a tortilla. It's a fucking abomination."

"Tony!" Pierre shouted. "I expect this behavior from your young friend, but from you? You should be ashamed of yourself, no?" Seems we were now first in line.

Tony turned his head. "Come on, Pierre. He had it coming, and every now and again a little sinner-abuse is good for the soul. You could probably stand to have a little fun yourself, right? I mean, this is a stressful business. Everyone needs to vent. Even the French, I bet."

The man continued to struggle under the water, flailing his arms, every now and again throwing a leg back, trying to catch Tony in the knee.

"You know I understand, Tony," sighed Pierre. "But now is not the time. I must get these people to their tables."

"I know. I know. But you can't blame a guy for wanting to let loose, right?" Tony released the man, who—being unaware of that fact that one can only die once, and he'd already filled his quota—immediately bent over at the waist and began gasping for air.

"I quite agree with you," Pierre said, "but it appears all you've let loose is that man's face into my koi pond." He pointed that finger of his at the pond, the koi nibbling at the edges of a seared, soggy, wrinkled mess of skin.

"Okay. Well, I am sorry about that."

Finally catching his non-breath, the man touched what used to be his face, now finding only muscle and bone. He leaned back over the pond, scooped out what remained of his face, and tried in vain to put it on, like it was a Halloween mask or something. When the skin slid back off his head and landed with a splat on the floor, he first looked at Tony, then Pierre, unsure of who to blame. He dug his cell phone out of his pocket and held it in the air, looking for service. "If I could leave a zero-star review of this place, I fucking would!" he shouted. "And then I'd burn it to the ground! I swear to fucking God!"

Pierre's expression never changed. He seemed no more annoyed than he had been with Tony only a moment ago. Like I said, a fucking professional, man. "Indeed, sir," he said. "But before you reduce our little establishment to embers, perhaps you will allow me the honor of showing you to your table?"

The man smiled—I think—like his table being ready was some sort of small victory over the staff. "About fucking time," he said, "and send a manager straight over. I'm gonna rip that fucker a new one."

"Of course, sir," Pierre said, smiling and pressing his button.

The curtain appeared. The man scooped up his face and walked through. The curtain vanished.

Tony wiped his hands dry on my back. "So where'd you send him first, Frenchy? Pride or Wrath?"

Pierre licked the tip of his finger and slowly turned a page in his ledger. "Neither, of course." He looked up with a sinister yet playful grin. "You have reminded me that one should be able to enjoy one's work, Tony. So first I have sent him see Luigi. He seemed, as you Americans would say, like a douche."

"My man!" Tony reached over the podium and punched Pierre in the arm. "I knew you still had it in you."

Pierre rubbed his apparently fragile arm. "*Oui*, Tony. I am the most fun. Now, if you do not mind…" He pressed his button, the curtain appeared, and he nodded in its direction.

"Oh. Of course. Sorry to hold you up. Let's go, kid."

I followed as Tony headed for the curtain, but I stopped at the podium. "Just one sec, if you don't mind, Pierre."

He glowered at me but allowed me to continue.

"Tony and I have to settle something. Where are all these people going?"

He sighed and looked over the line. "Gluttony, forty-eight. Lust, thirty-four. Pride, twenty-nine. Wrath—where I'll be counting that last gentleman, officially—twenty-one. Treachery, nine. One addition to the cleaning crew. And the slothful are only now beginning to arrive."

"Great," I said, swiping a mint and knowing I'd be catching shit from Tony. "Thanks."

Pierre cleared his throat. "A word of advice, if I may, sir?"

"Who doesn't love unsolicited advice? Whatcha got, Pierre?"

"It is unwise to test the gods," he said, nonchalantly going back to his ledger. "Is that not right, Tony?"

Tony turned up his palms and shrugged. "Look, man. I'm trying here, but I can't teach this kid a damn thing."

ELEVEN

Either they were beginning to figure out the issues with the doors, or I had become more accustomed to the void. It didn't feel like much time had passed by the time the lights came up.

If this was indeed a room, it was unlike any room I'd ever experienced. No walls that I could see—just miles of scorched earth stretching off to a dark horizon, like twilight, but infinitely more menacing. No ceiling, either. Instead, an eternity of rippling air, rising like heat off the concrete in July, up to swirling, fiery clouds. If there were night on the sun, it would feel like this place.

I doubt it would smell this way, though, the air heavy with ranch dressing—rancid, eons beyond the expiration date ranch that's been left spilt under the lowboy long enough that the Board of Health would surely close the place down.

I'd never liked ranch to begin with, but after decades of people asking for it with their fries and chips and fish and pizza and pretzels and breadsticks and bacon—and, believe it or not, even on their salads—ranch had become my utterly detestable arch nemesis. After one whiff of that shit, I didn't stand a chance.

Once I straightened back up and wiped my mouth with that back of my hand, Tony patted me on the back. "Jesus. I don't know how you still have anything in there. Thanks for keeping it off the shoes, though. You all right there, champ?"

I tried to say yeah, I was fine, but on the inhale all I got was more of that stinking condiment, and although I didn't puke again, it wasn't for lack of effort.

"Look, I know it's fucking foul," he said. "But you gotta get it together, ok? We're close, and, unbelievably, on time."

"Sorry, man," I said, covering my mouth and nose as best I could while catching my breath. "I just—fuck that's awful—we're close? It's like the surface of Venus out here—or, in here." I loogied out any remaining bile. "You know, nevermind. Which way? I gotta get away from that smell."

Tony grinned and tapped the tip of his nose twice with his index finger.

"What," I asked, mimicking the gesture, "does this mean?"

He did it again, this time flaring his rather sizeable nostrils to take a deep breath.

"I highly doubt this is an appropriate time for a cocaine break, Tony. Besides, I thought you were off that shit."

He dropped his hand back to his side. "Follow your

nose, asshole. We're headed towards the stench."

"But that's..." I caught myself and remembered where I was. "...exactly where we would be headed, wouldn't it?" I lowered my hand and took a few deep breaths, acclimating to the vile rankness that is my most despised condiment. "Lead the way, old man."

Tony did one more quick spot check of his shoes, nodded at me, and turned to his left. I turned to my right and walked alongside him. After about a minute of silence, I felt oddly calm. Other than the smell, heat, and ominously fiery-yet-somehow-dark clouds, this place wasn't so bad. And I don't really mean just this particular room, either.

It was like the whole place suddenly felt familiar. A stroll through The Inferno wasn't much different than a walk through the downtown restaurant district. Sinners everywhere. I can't begin to count all the gluttonous, lustful, wrathful, proud, and treacherous people I've ever met, how many of them I've passed on the street without so much as a nod. The only difference was that, here, the sinners were all grouped together, whereas up above, they just sort of milled about, bumping into each other and judging one another for each's particular brand of sin.

Here was order. Up there, chaos.

It was nice knowing what sort of shit we were about to walk into the moment Tony saw the room—a moment to mentally prepare is incredibly helpful in any situation. You don't always get that up there.

Up there you can never really tell what to expect. We don't each walk around with signs hanging from our necks that say things like *rapist* or *knowing how much they like ranch with their fries, still always forgets to order said ranch while ordering said fries.* We fucking should have the signs—we're all assholes in one way or another—but we don't. One of humankind's great failures, I suppose.

Anyway, I was lost in the middle of some fantastic self-actualizing, oblivious to all around me, when my left foot sunk too deep into some sort of warm sludge. I snapped out of my revelry and back into what I suppose would pass for reality, and I looked down to find I'd lost my ankle beneath a brownish film, like you might find on a vanilla Snack Pack that's been left open for a few weeks.

Fearing what the sludge might be, for this could not possibly be your plain old ordinary ranch, I gasped. And what I tasted—god help me, what I tasted in that air. I gagged just hard enough to produce one little mouthful of bile, which I spat into sludge, where it pooled on the surface for just a moment before it was swallowed by the film. If this had been earlier on our voyage, it would have been gallons of vomit, but I'm pretty sure that was the last of anything human I had in me.

I tried to yank my foot out of that nasty-ass shit, but I was suctioned in there good and tight, so I got my hands to my calf in the hope that some extra force might help.

"Whoa there, cowboy," Tony said, breaking my grip on my leg. "Hang on a sec."

I looked at him like *what the fuck, dude?*

"Don't freak out," he said, taking a step back. "You can totally just yank your foot right out of that shit. Just give me a minute." He reached inside his jacket and pulled a handkerchief from the pocket, handed it to me. "Might wanna hold this over your nose and mouth. And you should probably sit down first."

I gave him another *what the fuck* look, but sat down as instructed.

"I'm not gonna lie," he said, taking multiple steps back. "This won't be fun. But I think you should be fine."

"You think I should be fine!?"

Another step back. "Look, kid. No mortal's ever been in this situation, so no, I can't be completely sure. But yeah, I think you'll be okay."

"You're fucking with me, right?"

He put a hand to the back of his neck and rubbed a little. "Wish I could say so. Now, if I were you, I'd—"

I didn't want advice. I wanted out of the sludge. So I took and held a deep breath, freed my foot with a sickening squelch, and looked up at Tony, who had covered his nose and mouth with his hand and was now hauling ass away from me.

I went to call after him, like a fucking moron, but the release of my foot had opened a sizable hole in the film, allowing the true nature of the stench to reveal itself, filling my mouth, my nose, my lungs with the sort of rancid foulness that could only exist in Hell.

Through increasing dizziness, I caught a glimpse of my liberated foot, the death-ranch clinging like some sort of vomitous sap to my shoe, gravity pulling it slowly down. Then, I passed out.

For the second time today, I woke to find Tony

above me. "Snap out of it, kid."

I sat up, groggy and disoriented until the stench brought me back to life. "What the fuck, dude?"

"Hey," he said, standing back up and reaching out a hand to lift me from the ground, "I'm not the one who stepped in the shit. I told you it wouldn't be fun."

I took his hand and got to my feet. "Kind of a dick move running off like that, don't you think?"

"It's just self-preservation, kid. You don't survive thousands of years by sticking around for shit like that. Besides, you're fine, just like I said you'd be."

"Well bully for me," I said, for the first time surveying what it was I'd waywardly stepped into. It was a marsh, a seemingly endless brownish white marsh, dotted with innumerable round shapes that appeared to be steppingstones. And there were voices, thousands, hundreds of thousands of voices, all speaking over one another so I couldn't pick out a single word. I let my head drop and rubbed my temples. "We're crossing this, aren't we?"

"Finally figuring out the way things work here, huh?"

"Finally?! I feel like I caught on pretty quick there, you old prick." I took a step closer to the marsh and felt and heard the ranch squishing between my toes. The shoe, and the sock, had to go.

"I don't know if that's the best idea," Tony said, picking up my shoe, turning it upside down, and watching as the sludge dripped like snot to the ground. "You're gonna want to keep your toes covered for this part of the trip."

"Jesus fucking Christ," I said, peeling my saturated sock from my foot. "Next you're gonna tell me it's policy to wear closed-toed, slip-resistant footwear."

"Well yeah," he said, handing the shoe back to me. "I know it's Hell, but it's still a restaurant."

I shook the last drops of goop from the shoe. "Wouldn't want to get written up for a uniform violation." The shoe slid back on so easy I almost retched. "Let's just get this over with."

"Yeah. Let's do that." He walked a few paces down the solid ground before finding a suitable place to begin our crossing. "Another word of advice," he said, stepping onto the closest rock. "Don't believe a word any of these assholes has to say."

"What assholes? I don't see anyone."

"Take a good look at the steppingstones."

So I did, and they were not stones at all. They were heads, each turned towards the fiery clouds to keep the ranch out of their facial orifices, each of their mouths flapping endlessly. "Holy shit. So we're just walking on faces then."

Tony nodded.

I smiled unabashedly. "I'm totally down with that. And thanks for the advice about the shoes. Be a shame to lose a toe to the teeth of one of these fuckers, whoever they are."

"The Treacherous," Tony said. "I'm pretty sure I don't have to explain their sins."

I shook my head no.

"Well then," he said, carefully placing his first face-step, "let's get going."

I followed his lead, though not quite so carefully. I leapt from the shore onto my first face, and it felt every bit as amazing as I'd hoped. And now that I was so close, I could hear what those closest to me were saying.

"I've never dine-and-dashed in my life. I swear to god. Do I look like the kind of person who can't afford to go out to eat?"

"Why the hell would I need to steal those adorable little salt and pepper shakers from the table? It's not like I don't already have some at home."

"I'm telling you, my sister's a bartender. I know what she makes hourly. I'd never tell a tipped employee what a great job they did without tipping them properly. I mean, come on, compliments don't pay the bills, you know?"

They each had this constant stream of bullshit flowing from their upturned mouths. I stepped, jumped, leapt, and stomped more forcefully, and gleefully, with each face.

"I'm not sure this is supposed to be fun," Tony said, his spindly legs stretched out between two faces. "But hey, you do you, kid."

I landed heavily on two faces that were particularly close together and turned, smiling, to look at him. "I'm finally enjoying myself here, man. Don't fucking ruin it."

He nodded once. "You're right. Apologies."

"Damn right," I said, already looking for where to land my next punishing step. I found it quick but didn't immediately leap. I knew that face, knew the bullshit spewing from that mouth.

"Seriously," she was saying, "I mean, what kind of

person carries dead bugs around in their purse? How could anyone think I'd ever do something like that?"

If I weren't using my arms to maintain my balance, I'd have slapped my forehead with the surprise. "No fucking way."

Tony found some sturdy faces to stand on just to my left and laid a hand on my shoulder, possibly to steady me, but more likely to steady himself. "What you got?"

"I fucking know her," I said. "And I'm pretty sure she's talking about the night I caught her putting a dead cockroach on her salad. Like, she'd already eaten all of it except the last few bites, and as I was spieling this couple like three tables down, I watched her bend down all sneaky under the table, pull a little plastic baggie out of her purse, and drop something on her plate. Then when I went to check on her table, she was all like—"

"Stop right there, kid," he said. "You know I know the end of this story. You sure it's her?"

I looked at him like telling him I'd never been more certain of anything in my life. You never forget things like that, you know? Those moments when you can't believe a human being would dare to pull such shit on another human being? Right then, I wished I was wearing heels. Big heels. Like six fucking inches. Maybe heels of meat thermometers.

I readied myself to jump as high as I could, to land with as much force as my hundred- and eighty-pound frame would allow, but Tony forced me to stay put.

"Easy, tiger," he said. "I know how much you want to stomp the fuck out of her face—I do—but I think we can do better than that."

"I want to hurt her, Tony."

"I know," he said, taking his hand from my shoulder, "and we will. Just not physically." He held his hand out in front of him and used his Jedi, or possibly Sith, powers to lift her out of the ranch and slowly turn her to face him.

"You want out of here?"

"I don't belong here," she whimpered.

"I'm sure you don't. I mean, we all make mistakes, right?"

"We do," she cried. "I mean, we're only human."

"Right," Tony told her. "Lucky for you, there's a way out. All you have to do is be honest, just once. Admit what you did, and you'll never have to smell or taste ranch dressing again. Heaven loves a good penitent, you know."

Her face lit up and she didn't even have to think about it. "I—"

"No," he said, spinning her mid-air to face me. "Don't tell me. Tell him."

That waste of a human and I locked eyes, and I instantly realized she had no fucking idea who I was. She was in Hell because *I* caught her pulling that shit, *I* had her banned from that restaurant, and yet, to her, I was still just another faceless humanoid wearing a black apron over black dress clothes. *The help.*

"Look," she said, hovering in that haze of heat-rippled air, "I did it, okay? I ate free meals for years before some fucking kid caught me." She looked at him like she thought that was enough, but I knew, and was happy, that Tony wouldn't let her get away with that lame-assed, omissive confession. He didn't even have to say anything. He just looked at her, and then out came some more. "I carried dead bugs in a Ziploc bag in my purse. I put them in the food so I could complain and get a free meal." She looked at Tony. "Okay?"

He crossed his arms, harrumphed, and dangled her feet just above the surface-film of the marsh.

She sighed, defeated. "And I'd usually get extra free stuff, too, all right? Jesus. Gift certificates and free dessert cards and whatever. I went out like five nights a week, and I almost never paid for anything." Again she looked at Tony. I didn't, but I didn't need to; I knew what face he was making at her. "I didn't even tip." She took a breath. "I swear that's everything. I can go now, right?"

Tony looked at me and grinned, then back to her without losing that grin. "I believe you. Good work. You can definitely go." He raised his Jedi hand, and with it, her. "You can go right back to where you belong."

She beamed and clasped her hands together like saying thanks.

Tony dropped his hand to his side, and she plopped right back down into the ranch, her head dipping below the film and not resurfacing for a good five seconds, spitting thick, white-ish awfulness and looking to Tony for an answer to an unspoken but obvious question.

Tony got his balance right and grabbed my forearm for support as he squatted down so he could talk to her close. "Sucks, doesn't it? Being lied to?"

She opened her mouth to answer, but he sprung up

quick and smothered that shit with his bootheel. Then he looked at me. "Good?"

And god damn how good it really was, hearing her own it, watching her get absolutely nothing for her honesty. I grabbed him by the shoulders and forced him to look into my eyes—serious about this, I was. "Yeah. Good. Thanks, Tony."

He nodded once, hard, like *good*. "All right," he said. "Let's fucking go then."

The moment he removed his heel from her face, I launched myself as far as I could off my own face-rocks—which, in a place where the laws of physics as I know them behave, shall we say, differently, meant I was really high up there. When I finally landed square on my target, that deceitful waste of biological material, I heard things underfoot cracking and breaking, followed by a muffled and mumbled few syllables that could only mean a living sort of death. It was one of the best moments of my entire existence.

I looked at Tony, and he actually seemed scared, or at least startled. He started to speak, but I was so amped up that I cut him off.

"Move it, old man! We got somewhere to be!"

He stood there, his two feet muting two mouths, his own mouth agape.

I skipped across the rest of the heads like frolicking through a field of wildflowers and ended up on the far shore alone, my shoe still squishy, a smile still on my face as I waited for the powerful ancient being to catch the fuck up.

I turned my back to the marsh, surveyed my new

surroundings. The shore itself was the same dry, hot sand as where we'd started, but off in the distance I could see a patch of vibrant green. Very far off.

After a minute or so, Tony finally stepped off his last face, his foot hitting the firm ground with a familiar squish. "Disgusting fucking shit," he mumbled, shaking droplets of ranch from his pretty shoe.

I laughed, but when he looked at me I decided against giving him a hard time. It wasn't because he looked particularly angry, but because he suddenly looked old and tired, sick of this shit. Anyone who stays in the business too long eventually ends up looking this way.

"So," I said instead, thumbing back over my shoulder, "That's where we're going, right?"

Satisfied with the de-ranching, or at least giving up on it, Tony nodded. "That's the place."

"And what sort of hellacious demon spawn do we have to deal with on the way?"

"None, if you can believe it."

"Oh," I said, actually a little disappointed. "Well, let's go then, I guess. Anything I need to know about this GM?"

Tony shook his head no. "Just be yourself. You'll be fine." He walked past me, and as I turned to follow, he said, "At least, I fucking hope so."

I wasn't sure what he meant by that, but it didn't sound like it was about me anyway. This was about him, and we're all entitled to our own shit, so I let it be about him, and we walked towards the green.

TWELVE

One befouled foot apiece, we set off across the remaining hellscape. Each step carried us farther from the stench of the marsh and the unending noise pollution of millions of lying shitbags. Every second step squelched and gifted us with little puffs of rankness, olfactory reminders of where we'd just been.

"You'd think that after a few millennia, I'd remember exactly how nasty this shit is," Tony said, looking down to his spoiled foot. "Get a move on, kid. I gotta get this fucking boot off."

I had fallen a bit behind—dude's legs were like stilts, and he *really* wanted to get across that sand—so I quickened my steps. "Hey I'm trying here, man. But you're pretty fast for an old guy. No warp-drive this deep into Hell?"

"No warp-drive," he called, not slowing down to allow me to catch up. "Maybe I'll bring that up at the next staff meeting."

Even without the light-speed thing, we were quickly approaching the expanse of green. Now that we were closer, I noticed shapes on what I assumed was a lawn. A building no bigger than a garden shed stood just about in the center. Other shapes were dotted around the shed, but I couldn't really make them out. Frames and scaffolding, maybe. Or maybe a swing set, because why the hell not, right? By this point, nothing would have surprised me.

"No obnoxious questions about what we're gonna find up ahead?"

"Nope," I said, breathing heavily from trying to keep up. "I think I'm all questioned out."

"About fucking time." And I can't be sure, but I think he sighed with relief as he sped up, just in case I changed my mind.

I kept quiet and hoofed it after him until we got to the edge of the most immaculately manicured lawn I've ever seen.

"Oh, hell yes," Tony said as he kicked off his stinky, ranch-slicked boot and immediately set to peeling off his similarly saturated designer sock. He wiped the sole of his foot on the grass like getting rid of dog shit, and the grass wilted instantly, browning and shriveling into nothing, only to be replaced seconds later by fully grown, vibrant green blades. "Go ahead, kiddo. You know you want to."

I looked at my shoe—the faux-leather steaming, dissolving away—but still I hesitated. "I don't know, man," I said, instinctively balancing on my other foot, keeping the foulness off the grass. "Meeting the GM of

Hell with all my piggly-wigglies out feels a little unprofessional."

Tony removed his other boot and sock, tossing them unceremoniously onto the lawn. He wiggled his toes in the grass and smiled. "Damn that's nice. And trust me, barefoot is better than trudging that shit onto the carpet."

I shrugged and kicked off my own gross shoe, which landed maybe a foot from Tony's boots, which were now moving off over the grass, seemingly on their own, like the apple pie being carried off by ants at a cartoon picnic. "Um, Tony?"

He was still standing there, eyes closed and smiling as he molested the grass with his weirdly long toes. "Thought you said you were questioned out."

"I know," I said, "but, your boots. They're, uh, moving."

He looked but didn't seem surprised to see them walking off on their own. "It's not the boots that are moving, bud."

I watched the boots and thought for a moment. "Cleaning crew?"

Tony nodded. "Cleaning crew. Can't allow the GM's yard to be littered with ranch-covered flotsam, you know?"

I didn't bother to ask—like I said, I was all questioned out, you know? Besides, he'd already told me I'd learn about the apparently invisible cleaning crew. Instead, I set to freeing my other foot from its bonds, stepping barefoot onto the grass, and cooing like, I don't know, like something that coos. The grass was so fucking soft I couldn't help myself. No wonder Tony was still standing in the same spot, that stupid grin still on his face.

"Holy Jeebus," I moaned, "this is amazing."

"Right? Same as anywhere, being the boss has its perks." He looked away from me. "Just look at this place."

So I did, and I wasn't jealous, exactly, but it was close. To the left of the shed was a firepit encircled by patio furniture that I didn't even need to sit on to know it would have been like being supported by big, puffy clouds. To the right of the shed, the thing I thought might have been a swing set turned out to be a sort of glider, also apparently cloud-comfy.

"Damn, Tony."

"Right? There's a horseshoe pit out back, too. And a pond with a dock and a rowboat." He craned his neck to try to see around the shed. "At least, last time I was here there were, anyway. Kinda changes with his mood, you know?"

I didn't know, but I took his word for it. Again, no more questions.

Okay, maybe one more question... "Where's the office?"

"You don't really think that's a garden shed, do you?"

From the look of it, the shed, thin wood painted a cracking red like an old barn, would barely be able to hold us both, let alone an entire office. Like the entrance to The Inferno, the door was plain, decorated with only a rusty metal ring. Unlike the entrance to The Inferno, no creepy devil-mouth and no warning to abandon hope.

"So it's a TARDIS kind of situation, then? Fuckin' sweet."

"Well, it is definitely bigger on the inside," Tony said. "And time and space are kind of our bitches down here."

"Holy shit! All that crap about me being a nerd, and you're a fucking Whovian?! Hah! Who's your favorite Doctor?" I asked, getting excited about getting my geek on with Tony. "No wait—lemme guess. I bet it's—"

"Who wouldn't be a fucking Whovian?" he said with a nod. "But we'll compare notes later, yeah? We should go in."

"Damn right we'll compare notes," I said, still enjoying the feel of that smooth, soft grass massaging the soles of my feet, gently caressing the skin between my toes. And now I was looking forward to debating with Tony whether Daleks or Cybermen would be the more fearsome enemy. "Don't suppose we have time for a game of horseshoes first?"

"Hah. Maybe after. You ready?"

"Does it really matter?"

"No, it does not."

He got to the shed, grabbed the ring, which glowed the same red the one on the front door had, and pulled the door open. "Alright, kid," he said, gesturing for me to go through.

"Nah, that's cool," I said, waving him off. "After you."

He took a step away from the door but didn't release the handle. "There's no backing out now, you know. I mean, you're here, and you can't go back the way we came. Like I've said, the—"

"Yeah, yeah. The way out is through. I know. And I'm not trying to back out of anything. You're right. We came all this way, and I'm not even thinking about turning back. In fact, I'm sort of excited to meet the GM, see what this office is like, and call it a fucking night." I walked over, took the handle from him, and mimicked his earlier gesture. "I was really just being polite, Tony. For real. After you, man."

"Huh," he said, giving his feet one last rub on the grass. "Almost forgot what it felt like, someone being polite. Kind of frowned upon down here, you know?"

"Jesus Christ, Tony," I said, motioning for him to get a move on. "Don't go all mushy on me now, alright? I'm just holding the door, not carrying you over the fucking threshold."

"Oh fuck you." He stomped all surly through the door.

I allowed myself one last look at the yard, the desert beyond, the marsh beyond that. I took a deep breath and immediately dry heaved. Yeah, the place looked pristine and pure and everything, yet somehow the stench remained. After a moment to rub my watering eyes, I composed myself and followed Tony through the door.

It swung shut gently behind me, and I found Tony waiting in a fairly long hallway with fluorescent lights and cinderblock walls painted white. The frame around the only door, at the end of the hall, was a smaller replica of the main entrance. This devil-mouth, however, was painted a vibrant red, except for the menacing yellow eyes. The door itself was, well, just a door.

"Huh," I uttered as I walked, my feet slapping onto and suctioning off of the linoleum floor, to meet Tony halfway down the hall.

"Huh, what?"

"I don't know." I eyed the shoddy white paintjob and the long, humming bulbs overhead. "I was just expecting something, I don't know, a little more... grandiose, I guess?"

"I figured as much," he said, also looking around. "Honestly, nobody's really sure why this hallway is even here, or where it came from. Isn't even in the blueprints. I guess it's just that the bowels of all restaurants have a hallway like this, so, you know, here it is."

Crazy as this sounds, it made good enough sense to me.

"Anyway," Tony said as we got to the mini devil-mouth door, "here we are." He knocked twice, and the door opened.

"Tony!" a voice called from inside. "Get in here, you old sonofabitch!" The accent was German, or maybe Austrian. I've never been good with accents.

"On the way, boss," responded Tony. He then turned to me. "Remember, kid, there's nothing to worry about. Just be yourself."

I nodded, but in that sarcastic way a pubescent boy might when he's annoyed with his overinvolved father. "Yeah, we've been over this, Tony. Besides, you're the one who sounds nervous."

"If you say so, tough guy," he said as he walked past me into the office. "Close the door behind you."

I followed, but there was no need for me to close the door behind us, as it closed on its own. I paused to take in the room: a high ceiling, industrial chic, all exposed ductwork and I-beams, sheets of corrugated tin or what have you; an elegant chandelier type thing hanging at the center, blown-glass teardrops glowing red and orange around their bulbs; the walls papered a velvety textured blood red, the back wall decorated with various framed certificates and permits—occupancy restrictions, Board of Hellth certifications, and the like.

Aquariums lined the walls all around the room. Fucking huge ones, man—like each of them could have housed their own adolescent kraken, though in reality it looked like they contained millions of sea monkeys.

The floor was highly-polished black marble except for a swath of plush carpet that matched the wallpaper and ran through the center of the room, leading to two black leather armchairs that faced an old-as-fuck and beat-to-shit wooden desk that must have been a truly magnificent sight however many thousands of years ago it was made. On the desk: a desk lamp, one of those long, flat ones with a pull string and an opaque, red glass shade; a crusted and worn leather desk organizer with a paper calendar, decades in the place of days, centuries in the place of months; a quill pen in a jar of ink; a simple wooden humidor and a large ashtray.

By the time I made it to the desk, Tony had already taken a seat, crossed his legs, and settled in. "Grandiose enough for you?"

"Uh, yeah," was all I could muster.

"Well don't just stand there. Sit down, kid."

So I sat, and it may have merely been that we'd just finished a fairly arduous journey, but fuck me if that wasn't the most comfortable chair my ass has ever had the pleasure to sink into.

The chair on the other side of the desk faced away from us, and the man in the chair was on the phone. "They have just arrived. Have you finished seating the people from the restaurant fire? Well, certainly not the Slothful yet, of course. But everyone else? Excellent. Has maintenance finished repairing the doors? Wonderful. Send them to Pride. It would seem that something has caused my nephew to become excited. He'll need the distraction. Thank you, Pierre."

He put the phone in his jacket pocket—because of course the GM would have the only working cellphone—and spun in the chair to face us.

Wolfgang fucking Puck. I'd learned enough by now to know it wasn't the real Wolfgang Puck, just some trick of the eye or the mind or something, but still, Wolfgang fucking Puck.

"So good to see you, old friend," he said, reaching into the humidor to pull out three cigars. He handed one to Tony, set one on the desk, and lit the third for himself. "And I see you've managed to bring company."

Leaning back in his seat, Tony brought his cigar to his lips and caught the pack of matches Wolfgang tossed to him. "I told you I had a good feeling about him," he said before lighting up.

Wolfgang hit his cigar, blew a smoke ring. "Yes, I remember this. But I also remember you have said this of the others." He looked me over. "However, you did manage to get him to me. And in that tie, no less. Impressive." And then, with a wink, "Most impressive."

I straightened the TIE tie and my posture and began to speak, but with a wave of his hand I was silenced. And I don't mean the gesture got me to hold my tongue, either. My voice was stolen from me. I'd just been Ursula-ed by the GM of Restaurant Hell, Wolfgang not-fucking Puck.

"You will know when it is time for you to speak," he said.

Tony laughed. "Yeah, good luck with that, boss. Don't get me wrong, the kid's got potential, but he never shuts the fuck up. Jesus, the questions."

"Questions are a good thing, Tony. This is how we learn." He leaned over the desk and tapped the ash from his cigar. "You had many questions at first as well, if you remember. Like a child, you were. And now look what you've become."

"Yeah. Look what I've become." Tony reached for the ashtray, held. It was metal, possibly brass, and around the flat rim were the words *TAKING CARE OF BUSINESS*, framed on either side by lightning bolts. The base of thing read, in big block letters, *TCB!*, another bolt in place of the exclamation point. "Shit," Tony continued, "I missed Elvis?"

"I am sorry to say you did. I know how you like him. It seems the digital age is also causing problems in Music Hell, or Disgraceland, as he has taken to calling it. I could not help him as much as I'd hoped, but I was in need of a new ashtray, so I am happy he stopped by."

Tony set the thing back on the desk and went back

to being comfortable. "Anyway, like I said, the kid's got potential. I mean, sure, he talks *a fucking lot*, and he's got shit taste in fashion accessories, but he's got no love for these assholes, I can tell you that. And he's surprisingly tough. Don't let the tie fool you."

Wolfgang again looked me over. "You are certain?"

Tony uncrossed his legs and leaned forward. "Boss," he said, adding ash to the gift shop ashtray, "the kid's still mortal, and he survived stepping in the fucking Ranch."

Wolfgang leaned back in his chair, hit his cigar, and contemplated. "Impressive, indeed," he said, this time blowing a perfectly formed pitchfork. "But you must understand my position, Tony. Without question I trust your opinion. But I must in this case consider also your motives. So many you've tried to bring to me, and it has been an equal number of failures. Centuries you've been trying to leave here. As your friend, I understand, of course. But, as your employer, surely you understand I must consider this from many perspectives?"

Tony flopped back into his chair with a half-grunt/half-sigh. "Yeah," he said, ashing directly onto the carpet. "Of course I do."

"Come now, Tony. Do not get upset." He butted his cigar, pulled open a drawer, and removed one of those little green nets you use to scoop a goldfish from its bowl. "It is, after all, only business."

Tony hit his cigar and thought a long while. I know it was a long while because, having no voice in this conversation, I was left there to count the seconds and watch as Wolfgang walked over to an aquarium, scooped up some of the sea monkeys, and dumped them on the floor.

"I know it's just business," Tony finally said, "but we both know I've been a trusted and loyal employee for, fuck, seven thousand years now?"

"I'd have to check your file," said Wolfgang, settling back into his chair, "but that sounds close enough."

"Fucking right it's close enough. And I'm not trying to pull one over on you, boss. Sure, the kid's a little annoying, but he's perfectly capable, and I've put in my time and then some."

They both looked at me then, like they'd forgotten I was in the room.

Wolfgang relit his cigar. "I trust you have not told him?"

"You told me not to tell any of them, so I haven't."

"Of course you have not. And you are right, old friend. I have never placed more trust in an employee, and you have never failed me. I suppose it is time," he said, raising his hand in my direction.

Tony leaned forward and raised his hand like *stop*. "You might wanna keep his voice until after you tell him. I'm not joking about all the questions and talking. Take the silence while you still can."

Wolfgang frowned and lowered his hand. "Perhaps you are right," he said to Tony. Then, to me, "Child, what I am about to tell you will be difficult to understand, but—"

I stood up and headed straight back down that red carpet for the door. I'd put up with enough already—not only tonight, but in all those years as the faceless help—

that if I wasn't going to be allowed to speak, I was finished allowing them to speak to me.

Tony jumped out of his seat after me, grabbed me by the shoulders, and spun me around to face him. "Where do you think you're going? We talked about this, kid. There's only one way out, and it's not back that way."

I looked him in the eye for a few moments before making all sorts of violent gestures I hoped would get my point across.

He understood. "This might be a bad idea, boss," he said, still looking at me, "but maybe you should let him speak."

"You are certain?"

"Well, not really, no. But I guess this is when we'll find out if I'm right about him or not." He looked at me, and I knew I'd been right—he was nervous as fuck. To his credit, though, I believed him when he said, again, quietly so only I could hear, "Just be yourself, kid. You'll be fine."

I turned to face the fake Wolfgang. As I did, he waved his hand, and my voice returned to me.

I didn't waste a single second. "First off," I said, pointing a finger at the GM, "Fuck you for taking my voice. And second," spinning that finger so close I nearly took out Tony's left eye, "fuck you for thinking I don't know when I'm on a working interview. I don't give a fuck how fucking old you are. Or even what you are. Immortal, incorporeal, or fucking otherwise, you're still a fucking dick."

I was hoping my vitriol would have produced a

different response, but Tony merely grinned. It was very disappointing.

"What do you think you know, child?" Wolfgang asked, again relighting his stogey.

I approached the desk and noticed that Tony's chunk of cigar ash was being carried off just as his shoes had been. I paused a moment, but I wasn't about to let it distract me. "I know that Tony's trying to leave his job, and apparently has been for a *very* long time. And I'm pretty sure we could have just come straight to see you instead of going through all those, ahem, *dining rooms*. But if someone's gonna work in a place, they're gonna have to know the lay of the land, right? And I'm pretty sure up there I'm dead, or at least dying." I turned to face Tony. "That country boy really fucked me good, huh?"

The grin was gone from Tony's face. He nodded. "Yeah. Sorry kid."

"Smart, this one," said Wolfgang. "Sit, child, and please calm down. Here." He handed me that third cigar and a pack of matches—*TCB!*; must have come with the ashtray. I sat and lit up while Tony settled back into his chair.

"All you have said is true," Wolfgang went on. "I must apologize for the deception, but over the years we have found this is the best way to introduce a mortal to Hell. The human mind, it is a tricky thing."

I exhaled, not even trying for the smoke ring because I've never been able to make one. "Can't argue with you there," I said. "But seriously? This is the best way to introduce a mortal to Hell? What about all the sinners? They seem to be taking it, uh, fine I guess."

"It's different with a live human," Tony chimed in. "Or, one who's in transition. The first couple we brought in, their heads, quite literally, exploded. Too much information at once. Too much, well, everything. Took some trial and error, but eventually we figured out the tour was the best way to go."

I hit my cigar and contemplated. "But you said I was the first one to make it all the way here."

He reached over and put his hand on my shoulder. "Congratulations, kid. Wanna hear what you've won?"

I brushed his hand off. "I'm assuming I've won your job, yeah?"

"Yeah."

"And you know what I'm gonna tell you to do with it, right?"

"Yeah."

"And yet, here we are. Why?"

"You are in the process of dying," Wolfgang said, rolling his cigar between his thumb and middle finger. "We cannot help this. Nor can we force you to take Tony's position. The choice is yours, and yours alone."

I got the feeling I couldn't exactly trust Wolfgang, him being the GM of Hell and all, so I turned back to Tony. "What happens if I turn down the job?"

"Well," he said. "You die, and you end up where you end up."

"And where might I end up?"

"One of the Heavens or one of the Hells. And you're not gonna want to hear this, but almost nobody gets into the Heavens."

I reached for the ashtray, but I'd waited too long,

and an inch of ash fell first onto my foot and then to the floor. "Sorry about that. Cigars aren't usually my thing," I said to Wolfgang. Then, back to Tony, "But you're saying there *is* a chance I can get into one of the Heavens though, right?"

They both found this fucking hilarious. Once they stopped laughing, Tony wiped the tears from his eyes. "I want you to think, kid. You've been in the industry your entire adult life, right? Twenty, twenty-five years?"

I nodded.

"Yeah. You might not be coming to this Hell, but there's no way you're making it into one of the Heavens."

I crossed my arms like I meant business. "And who are you to say where I'll end up?"

"Come on, kid," Tony said, butting out his own cigar. "Think back on your life. All of it. Sure, you aren't slated to come here, but remember, this is only one of thousands of Hells. Do you really think you're not guilty of at least one cardinal sin?"

So I thought about it, and it didn't take long to reach a conclusion. I, like just about anyone else I'd ever met, was indeed a fucking asshole. No way Heaven was in the cards for me. "But what about, you know, like the forgiveness of a merciful God or whatever?"

Again with the laughing.

"I am glad you had me return his voice," Wolfgang finally said. "The child is funny."

I wanted to be angry, but all I felt was defeat. Well, defeat, and a slight tickle on my bare feet. I looked down and saw bits of ash moving off, seemingly on their own. I picked up my right foot and pointed at it. "And what the fuck is this, anyway?"

"It is the cleaning crew," answered Wolfgang.

"I figured that, *boss*. But I mean, you know, I could use the details."

Wolfgang pulled a magnifying glass from a drawer, stood, and motioned for me to come with him. When we got to one of the aquariums, he handed me the magnifying glass. "See for yourself."

I hunched down, raised the glass to my eye, and saw god knows how many tiny little human bodies, all dressed in black. They were mostly motionless, just a twitch here or there as they were suspended in a liquid I was pretty sure contained some percentage of slug juice. "Fuck me," I said. "Who are these poor schmucks?"

Tony had made his way over. "Food service workers who were also shitty enough customers to have found their way here. Those who really should have known better."

I leaned closer, trying to see if I recognized anyone, but they were just too tiny. "And the water?"

"Not merely water, of course," said Wolfgang, resting a hand on my shoulder. "It has been infused with milk from my niece."

I straightened back up and handed the magnifying glass back to him. "That's what I was gonna guess, actually. Why's it making them twitch?"

They started back towards the desk, and I followed. Once we were all back in our respective chairs, Tony answered, "You know those dreams when you're at work and no matter how often you refill all the water glasses, they never actually fill? Or your section keeps getting sat over and over again without end? Some people call them *wait-mares*? When they're in the goop, it's a constant waitmare. And when they're not in the goop, they're cleaning up blood and acidic spittle from Wrath, or all manner of foulness from the club in Lust, or when Paulina takes a shit in Gluttony..." He trailed off and turned a little green at the thought, but shook his head and snapped out of it. "Well, these are those assholes who sit down, say *oh, I'm a server, too*, and proceed to be just the fucking worst. It's my favorite of all the punishments, actually."

"Damn right," I said. "Fuck those guys."

"Yes, yes. Fuck those guys, indeed," said Wolfgang. "But I am afraid we are running out of time. I have another appointment I must prepare for. If you would like some time to—"

"I'll take the job," I said, cutting him off.

"Seriously?" Tony asked with a befuddled look. "Just like that?"

"Well, it's not really just like that," I said, relighting my cigar. "I've been doing this front of the house shit for a long time, you know? Long enough that a lot of what I've seen here hasn't been really any worse than what's gone on in my head for at least the last decade, anyway. Not that I've ever considered this as the next step in my professional career, but like you said, there's no fucking way I'm getting into any sort of Heaven. And you said it's been like seven thousand years for you, right? I know that's a damn long time, but it beats a literal eternity of torture and pain. Plus," I said, realizing exactly how true it really was, "I've never really liked it up there, anyway."

Tony nodded. "Who does, really? But still, you're

gonna want to make sure you're, you know, sure about this."

"I'm sure it'll feel like any other job, eventually. I'll enjoy watching these fuckers get their due for at least a couple thousand years, then I'll get bored and start looking for something new. Maybe I'll find my own replacement and come join you in retirement."

"Excellent," said Wolfgang. He dug into the desk, brought out a piece of paper, and slid it and the quill pen to me. "All that is left is to sign the contract, and then you will begin your training with Tony."

I looked at the paper. *Contract of Employment for The Inferno*, it read, *details to be determined*. I paused at the *to be determined* thing, but only for a moment—no position I'd ever taken had completely fit the job description. I dipped the quill into the ink and signed my name. The paper went up in a puff of flame and smoke.

"It is done, then," Wolfgang said. "Welcome to The Inferno, child. And Tony, my friend, congratulations. You have earned this." He took his phone back out and started dialing. "Now please take him to Pierre, get him some shoes—and a grownup fucking tie—and get him in the system."

Tony stood and shook his, our, boss's hand. "You got it, boss. Come on, kid. Let's go."

I stood and followed him to the door. "I thought you said we couldn't get back this way."

Tony grinned and pushed open the door. There, on the other side, where the void should have been, was the waiting room.

Pierre paid the long line of sinners no mind. Phone

pinned between his shoulder and ear, shit-eating grin on his face, he held a pair of scissors in one hand and a classy, blood-red necktie in the other. "I have just been informed of the news," he said, allowing the receiver to fall from his shoulder and hang dead at the end of its cord. "Congratulations, Tony. I know you have been working at this for some time, *mon ami*."

Tony smiled and sighed like the weight of the underworld had finally been lifted from his shoulders. "Thanks, Pierre. I never thought I'd see the day."

"Nor I," Pierre said. Then, turning to me, "And you, welcome to the staff. I trust you are ready to begin your training?"

"Like, right now?"

Tony slapped me on the back. "The sooner the better, kid. Don't get me wrong, surviving the interview process is one hell of an accomplishment, but it'll take a lot longer than two weeks to get you ready for the actual job."

"How long do I—"

"I was in training half a century before I worked a shift on my own, and I was born down here. I'll be amazed if you're ready in three times that." I must have made some kind of face, because he felt the need to continue. "Don't worry though. Time down here is wibbly-wobbly, remember? It'll feel like the blink of an eye."

"Fifteen-hundred years?" I asked, punching him in the arm, friendly-like. "You sure you can handle being around me that long?"

He punched my arm in return, friendly-like, though

it still knocked me back into Pierre's podium. "Luckily," he said, "it'll feel like the blink of an eye for me, too."

I pushed myself off the podium and straightened up. "Well then yeah, let's get started."

"Wonderful," Pierre chimed in. "First thing is first, no?"

"First thing?"

"Here at The Inferno, we take great pride in our professionalism." He held the scissors out in front of me, presenting them like they were a fucking dessert tray. "As thoroughly as I would enjoy the honor, I feel it is only right to allow you to deal with that tie yourself."

"Oh. Right." I took the scissors in one hand and held my TIE tie out in front of me with the other, but then I hesitated.

Tony rested a hand on my shoulder. "The only way out is through, kid."

With one snip, the tie fell to the floor.

"And now," Tony said, "begin your training, we can."

Daniel Parme is the author of *Hungry* (a novel of sex, drugs, and cannibalism), *Post* (a dystopian novella), and *Confluence* (a more literary affair). He is the fiction editor at After Happy Hour Review and has been working in food service for a very, very long time.

Printed in the USA
CPSIA information can be obtained
at www.ICGtesting.com
CBHW030839011124
16733CB00023B/633